Kimba

Geoffrey Malone spent most of his childhood in Africa and avoided any formal education until the age of eleven. After school in England, he spent sixteen years as a soldier, then joined a Canadian public relations firm in Toronto. During all this time, he travelled widely and developed a fascination with animals in the wild. He returned to Britain in 1991, determined to become a children's author.

He has written six books for children, each one with a powerful and closely-observed animal interest. His story of a fox, *Torn Ear*, won the 2001 French Children's Book of the Year Award and the Prix Enfants grands-parents Européen. In England, *Elephant Ben* was shortlisted for the 2001 Stockton Children's Book of the Year Award.

In *Kimba* Geoffrey Malone uses his own experience of life in the wild to describe how a lion cub learns to survive on the merciless plains of East Africa.

Kimba

GEOFFREY MALONE

*Hodder
Children's
Books*

a division of Hodder Headline Ltd

A Catalogue record for this book is available from the
British Library

ISBN 0 340 86058 8

Typeset by Palimpsest Book Production Limited,
Polmont, Stirlingshire

Printed and bound in Great Britain by
Bookmarque Ltd, Croydon, Surrey

Hodder Children's Books
A Division of Hodder Headline Ltd
338 Euston Road
London NW1 3BH

To my sister, Julia

One

Sabba's cubs were born in the early afternoon. It was the lioness's first litter and the sound of her purring filled the den she had made, high up amongst the boulders of M'goma Hill.

There were three of them. Bewildered little creatures with wobbly legs and mottled brown coats: essential camouflage against ever-watchful predators like leopards or hyenas. It would be a week before they could see and six months until the spots started to fade.

Sabba held them in turn between her paws and washed them with a long, pink tongue. The cubs tried to squirm away, wrinkling their noses in tiny snarls and yowling in protest. But she held them firm and inspected them. They were even more furious when she rolled them over on to their backs and cleaned the fluffy white fur of their undersides. They hissed in temper and raked at her chin with ridiculously large paws.

Sabba purred with pride and rubbed her face along their tiny bodies, delighting in their warmth and scent. She put her head against their chests and marvelled at the beat of their tiny hearts. They were blind and helpless and vulnerable. But they were hers. A fierce tenderness filled her and she crooned to herself in utter contentment. She closed her eyes and her head drooped. She was tired from the birth and glad it was all over. She yawned and lay down.

But the cubs were hungry and already demanding to be fed. In their blindness, they tried to clamber over her forepaws to get to her. They jostled and struggled and kept losing their balance and rolling back on the ground again. Sabba watched, entranced.

When their cries became impossible to ignore any longer, she lifted them up by the scruff of the neck and placed them alongside her. The male cub was the first to feed. Sabba listened to his little sighs of pleasure. She noticed the shape of his head and the determined way in which he fed. Her purring grew louder. She called him Kimba, which is the sound the evening breeze makes in the long grass when it is time to go hunting.

She sensed that if he survived, he would one day be as strong and as powerful as Black Mane, his sire and the leader of the pride. But his chances of doing that were, at best, unlikely. Very few male lions lived for more than four years. Life on the plains was merciless and uncertain for animals of all kinds, including lions.

The night before the cubs were born, she had lain here in the darkness of the cave and listened to Black Mane roaring. He had sounded bad-tempered and hungry. And she knew why. Food was scarce at this time of year. It was the middle of the dry season and most of the grass had already been eaten. The great herds of zebra and wildebeest had moved away and the plains were becoming dust bowls.

Now the only prey the lions could find were small antelopes like the Steinbok. There were always warthogs but that meant hours of digging to get them out of their burrows. Occasionally, the lions would find an old buffalo in the reeds along the river. Then there would be enough meat for all of them.

Black Mane's pride were not the only animals who

needed meat. There were other prides, jealous of the size of their territory and quick to take advantage of any loss of vigilance. There were hyenas and wild dogs who hunted in packs fifty strong. They were the most feared predators of all and had even been known to attack lions.

There were leopards too. Cunning hunters who waited in the tops of trees or on rocky outcrops like M'goma and watched for their prey. It was good country for them. Sabba had seen their claw marks slashed across the bark of the fever trees in the valley below the hill.

But until the rains came and the grass grew again they would all go on being hungry.

During the last migration, there had been times when the pride had killed three times in as many hours. Gorged with meat, they had afterwards found shade and slept soundly for the next two days.

Sabba had been away for almost a week looking for a den. She had finally chosen the cave because there was only one approach: a narrow twisting path that plunged downwards between vertical slabs of rock. She had prowled round the hill listening and watching for enemies. When she was satisfied, she had gone inside and had her cubs.

Sabba was just four years old but already she was a more skilful hunter than either of her half-sisters. She could tell from Black Mane's roaring just how much the pride were missing her.

She had a very clear understanding of how zebra or impala thought. Out hunting, she could anticipate the way even the most wily of them would swerve and twist and double back. Only Meru, her mother and the matriarch of the pride, was wiser. But she was getting old now and when she stayed at the back of the hunt with Black Mane, the others were content to let Sabba take the lead.

Remembering the taste of fresh meat, Sabba swallowed hard and put the thought out of her head. Her cubs were the only thing that mattered. For the next two months, Sabba and her little family would be entirely on their own. Only when the cubs were big enough to keep up with the pride, would she take them back and show them to Black Mane and Meru and the others.

She watched the cubs until they had finished feeding. They fell asleep almost at once, too sleepy even to complain when she licked their faces and ears. The lioness stared down at them lying with their heads on her flank and sighed in happiness.

11

The sound of her purring grew louder in the great stillness that covered the land.

It was the hottest part of the day when even the lizards hid from the blistering strength of the sun. They slipped into the deep fissures between the rocks and waited until it was safe to come out. On the plain below, snakes lay in loose coils deep inside termite mounds and panted. The mountains at the edge of the plain had long since disappeared behind a quivering curtain of haze.

The sky was a vast grey bowl under which nothing moved. Nothing but the fine red dust that sifted through the branches of the thorn trees and fell slowly on to the parched ground beneath.

Two

Sabba did not leave her cubs for a moment during the next two days. Not until she was sure there were no predators lying in wait nearby. When she was not feeding the cubs, she stood inside the entrance to the cave, listening and testing the air for the smallest sign of danger.

Hyenas were the most numerous predators and among the most ruthless. They also had the strongest jaws of any animal on the plain. Sabba had watched a pack of them fighting over an elephant carcass, cracking open the massive leg bones to get at the marrow inside.

It was hyenas who would probably kill her one day, that is if she lived long enough. They killed most lions that managed to survive into old age. Sabba had seen them tormenting an old lioness too lame to keep up with her pride. They had circled round and round her for days, snapping at her and giving her no rest, waiting until she was too weak to fight them off any longer.

Sabba also remembered all the solitary male lions who roamed the plain, hungry and aggressive. They were either too young to have a pride of their own or had been driven away from their own by a stronger challenger. Black Mane was always chasing them off the pride's territory. None of them would have any hesitation in devouring another male's cubs.

It was thirst, finally, that forced Sabba to leave the cave. The cubs were fast asleep, lying with their paws around each other's necks. She stooped over them and listened to their quiet breathing. Reassured, she padded silently to the entrance of the cave and slipped out into bright moonlight.

The air was warm and full of wonderful scents. Sabba took a deep breath and savoured them. She unsheathed her claws and stretched. It was a long, sensuous movement that brought the blood tingling in her veins. For a moment afterwards she felt dizzy. Her muscles were stiff and cramped and her body still felt sore. Then the feeling passed and she gave a low growl of satisfaction. She squatted down and marked the ground in warning.

It was good to be outside and back in her world again. But first, she had to be completely sure there was no lurking menace to the cubs. She leapt up on to a rock and sat there like a gigantic cat. The night was alive with the familiar sounds of animals living and dying.

Like all her kind, Sabba's hearing was exceptional. A hundred metres away, a pair of bush rats were searching a dead tree for grubs. She could hear the rasp of their claws and their excited squeakings as they tore the bark away.

Two miles beyond, on the other side of the river, a warthog snorted in triumph. Sabba remembered the taste and swallowed painfully. Warthogs were delicious to eat and easy to bring down. She listened again and thought she heard the sound of stones clinking. The pig would be digging at the base of a tree, searching for roots or tubers. She narrowed her eyes, concentrating on the noise and trying to pinpoint exactly where it was coming from. If the warthog had found food and was busy digging it up, it would be fully absorbed in its task and easy prey.

But first she must drink.

Sabba slipped down between the rocks and over a scree of small stones at the bottom. She made no sound. She waited beside a bush for a further minute and all the time the smell of water grew stronger. She waited there motionless until she could bear it no longer. Her thirst was suddenly unbearable and she began to run. The next moment, she was racing for the river: a bounding ghost hardly disturbing the dust underfoot.

Sabba had chosen M'goma Hill from a dozen similar kopjes for another good reason. There was water nearby. Like the others, M'goma was rocky, steep-sided and covered with scrub. But less than a mile away, springs from deep underground fed a number of streams which joined to form a slow-moving river. Although the sun had reduced it now to a series of long muddy pools, it never completely dried up. As a result, it was a magnet for wildlife while the thick undergrowth along its banks gave predators perfect cover.

Sabba went down the bank and picked her way across the churned-up mud. She crouched down at the water's edge and drank greedily. New strength began to spread through her body. She drank until her stomach felt bloated. But all the time her eyes never left the surface of the river. There had been crocodiles here during the last big rains and she had seen what they were capable of.

When she could drink no more, she lay up in the bushes along the river bank and groomed herself. She cleaned splashes of mud from her belly and legs and tried unsuccessfully to remove a tick from her shoulder.

Then she remembered the warthog and sat up to get her bearings. Sabba had drunk too much and felt heavy and uncomfortable. She needed to kill quickly and get back to the cubs. She would feed at the kill itself and not drag it back. There must be no tell-tale smears of blood anywhere near the den.

She crossed the river. It was shallow and barely reached her stomach. It didn't take long to find the place where the warthog had been digging.

Freshly dug earth and chewed remains of vegetation were strewn across the ground. She followed the warthog's scent for a hundred metres then, in the middle of a gully, suddenly lost interest.

She had picked up something far more exciting. Sabba scratched the ground to get at the scent. It was the unmistakeable smell of impala. She began to circle round, turning her head from side to side, testing the air. She was desperate to find where it had gone.

She found hoof marks in a patch of deeper sand and this gave her the lead. She began to follow the tracks, moving forward at a quick walk. Minutes later she found the place where it had stopped to mark territory. The ground under the bush was still damp. It was a young buck, physically mature and on its own.

Some distance further on, the impala had stopped to graze. The sand was scuffed and there were fresh droppings.

And then she saw it, standing in the open between two dense patches of thorn bush. It was looking back along the way it had come, looking directly at her. Sabba froze, not moving a muscle.

The impala was suspicious. It kept shifting its weight from foot to foot, bracing itself for instant flight. It tossed its head and the moonlight threw long shadows from its horns across the bare ground.

It was thirty metres away. Much too far for any lion to risk charging it. Impalas were fast animals. They could leap ten metres at a time. Sabba needed to get in much closer to have a chance of taking it.

She kept perfectly still and waited. Eventually the

antelope stopped shivering and began to feed again. Sabba sank down behind a straggly bush until her belly brushed the ground. The tip of the lioness's tail twitched in anticipation as she studied the ground. There was a large acacia tree fifteen metres upwind of the buck. If she could only get to that without being seen, it would make a good place to attack from.

Then she noticed a shallow fold in the ground running towards the tree. It wasn't ideal but it would give her some cover. To reach it she would have to back out very slowly from behind the bush.

She was just about to move, when a tiny movement caught her eye. It was a snake. A big one and very close. She watched its tongue flicker out again. Then, with a flowing movement of its coils, it slithered across the ground in front of her. Sabba's lips drew back in a silent snarl.

Immediately, the snake's head swung towards her. It was a spitting cobra, well over a metre long and as thick as a man's arm round the middle. Its tongue searched the air again and found the sudden warmth of Sabba's body heat. The cobra stopped and reared up. It hissed and its hood began to inflate.

The lioness was rigid with fear. She knew exactly the danger she was in. One wrong move and the cobra would spit at her. It would aim for the shine in her eyes and deliver its venom like the blast from a sawn-off shot gun. A small drop of that poison would be enough to blind her for the rest of her life. The cobra was far too close for Sabba to risk swiping at it with a paw. She was helpless.

All she could do was keep utterly still and hope the snake would lose interest. A full minute passed. The snake's head swayed in front of her as if tempting her to make a move. Somehow, Sabba kept her nerve.

Slowly, very slowly, the cobra began to close its mouth. It lowered its head and sank down. Gathering its coils together, the snake continued on its way towards the nest it had made in a nearby heap of rocks. Sabba watched it slide out of sight and blew out her cheeks in relief. She shivered and felt weak. Only then did she remember the impala.

She peered through the bush again and saw that the buck was still there. It was feeding contentedly with its back towards her.

The light was changing. Sabba looked up and saw the moon was about to go behind a cloud. There was no need now to bother with the aca-cia tree.

She waited a moment longer until the shadow

reached the impala, then she was out in the open, running fast towards it, her body hugging the ground. Every muscle tensed in excitement.

Twenty metres away, the impala reached for a higher bunch of leaves. Sabba came at a run, now bunching the muscles in her back legs ready to leap. A split second later, the impala saw her and screamed. It leapt high into the air in terror. And in that moment, Sabba covered four metres in a single bound.

But it was not enough and Sabba knew it. Whether it was because of the birth or the amount of water she had drunk, she was struggling to find the extra speed she needed. The impala bolted between the thorn bushes with the lioness in hot pursuit. The buck twisted and jinked, dodging between ant hills and rocks, its eyes rolling and a white froth gathering at the corners of its mouth. Sabba followed every twist and turn the buck made, driving herself after the bobbing tufts of hair at its heels. Yet somehow, it always stayed just out of reach.

The buck was strong and showed no sign of tiring. Sabba made a final despairing leap to try and trip the animal's back legs with her paw. She was a fraction too late and one of the impala's razor-sharp hooves instead struck her in the shoulder. Sabba crashed to the ground.

She slid on her side for twenty metres. When the dust settled, she was still winded and lay there for a while longer. She got to her feet and felt the muscles in her shoulder beginning to stiffen. She turned and slowly made her way back home, every limb in her body aching. It seemed an age before Sabba got back to M'goma and dragged herself up to the den.

When she got there, the cubs were wide awake and demanding milk. Painfully, Sabba lay down and let them feed. She was hungry and tired. She gave a grunt of discomfort and stared into the darkness. Tomorrow she must eat.

Three

Kimba lay in wait behind a tuft of grass, watching his sisters tussle over a piece of stick. Kitu, the smaller one, had seen it first. She had been lying happily on her back, rolling the stick between her paws, when Wheen pounced.

Kitu was on her feet in a flash, snarling in rage. She swatted Wheen hard in the face with a paw and snatched the twig back. Wheen reared up on her hind legs and the two of them swayed backwards and forwards, biting furiously at one another.

Kimba's eyes were wide with excitement. He knew Wheen would win in the end. She always did. She was heavier and more determined. He waited until Wheen had forced Kitu to the ground, then leapt on her back, biting at her neck. All three of them rolled over in a squirming heap until the stump of a tree brought them up short. They separated, the game at an end, and sat side by side grooming themselves.

Kimba noticed a dung beetle hurrying over the sand in front of them and pounced. He lost it in the dust. Kitu gave a growl and hooked it back from under a root with her paw. The beetle landed on its back and frantically waved its legs in the air. Wheen snapped at it. Kimba pushed her away and the next moment all three of them were rolling over once again.

Sabba listened to the commotion below her for a moment then, satisfied, went back to scanning the plain for any signs of the pride. The sun climbed higher and she felt its strength burning into the back of her head. If she was going to rejoin the pride, then the sooner she started the better. The cubs would feel the heat badly enough as it was.

She knew the pride was not too far away. Just before dawn, she had heard Black Mane and Meru begin to roar. Soon afterwards the other two lionesses – her half sisters – joined in. They roared like this on most nights, usually just before the dawn. It was a sound full of menace and the antelopes grazing in the grey half light tossed their heads and quivered. It was a warning to other lions to keep off their territory and it lasted for half an hour or more. Often, they would hear other lions roaring.

Sabba guessed her pride had made a kill during the night and would soon be sleeping it off. She was sure they would head for a clump of shady acacia trees a couple of miles to the west. And that would be quite far enough to risk taking the cubs.

At nine weeks, the cubs were old enough now to keep up with her. Last week, she had taken them to a kill she had made in the reeds by the river. They had squatted down beside the carcass and fed for themselves while she kept watch. They were ready now to join the others. The sooner they all got started the better.

She studied the ground carefully and chose a route that would take them clear of the thickets by the river bank. A cub could easily stray along there and be at the mercy of whatever predator might be lurking.

She gave a short growl and came leaping down from the rocks. The cubs ran to her, rubbing their heads against her chin in affection. Kitu tried to suckle but soon stopped when Sabba snarled at her. The lioness licked the top of their heads in turn and without a backward glance, set out down the gully. The cubs followed in a ragged line with Kimba leading.

It was wonderful fun for the cubs who by now were becoming very bored spending so much time playing round the cave. Brilliantly coloured birds flew just ahead of them, darting from branch to branch. Kimba jumped up at one of them, trying to catch it in his mouth. It flew off with a shrill scream that set the other birds protesting loudly.

At one point, they came across a column of ants carrying a dead centipede back to their nest. Wheen scrabbled at them with her paws. Kitu joined in. She seized the centipede in her mouth but dropped it when hundreds of enraged ants swarmed into her mouth and nostrils. She spent the next hundred metres sneezing and spitting them out.

Sabba ignored their antics. She walked at a steady pace, listening intently for any sign of danger. Occasionally, she looked round to make sure the cubs were keeping up.

She checked her stride only once in front of a small thorn bush. Deliberately she turned to one side to avoid it. This puzzled Kimba. It looked just like any other small bush and they had passed hundreds of them already. What was so different about this one?

But he followed her example and skirted it by a long body length. As he passed the bush, he looked down. It took him a couple of seconds before he could make out the shape of the head in the dust and the black, unwinking eyes of the puff adder watching him.

Puff adders he learnt later, were especially dangerous. They were heavy, powerful snakes with very long fangs on the upper jaw. Their bite would penetrate most animals' skins, including a lion's. They were also very hard to kill from behind as they could turn their heads through 180 degrees.

Away from the river, the ground became more broken. Soon they were crossing steep-sided ravines littered with small rocks which hurt the cub's feet. It was while they were walking up one of the bigger gullies, that they suddenly came face to face with a pack of wild dogs.

Sabba stopped dead. Kimba, who had been plodding after her and not looking where he was going, bumped into her back legs. The lioness flung a glance over her shoulder for a way out but by then it was too late. The dogs had seen them.

Sabba bunched her neck into her shoulders and gave a huge snarl. Kimba's eyes widened. He had never heard her snarl like this before. They must be in great danger from these strange looking animals.

There were eleven of them with splotchy yellow, black and white coats. They were scrawny and battered looking with cunning eyes. Yet, though small, they were probably the most feared killers on the plains. They hunted in disciplined packs and could run all day. Their coats were easy to see at long distances and this allowed the pack to see each other during a hunt.

Their favourite method of attack was for the leader to leap up and seize the prey by the nose and then hang on while the others closed in and tore open the belly and the soft skin between the legs. They would then rip the animal to pieces while still alive.

Wild dogs mainly hunted in daylight so that they very rarely came into direct conflict with lions. But Sabba had watched them out hunting many times and knew what they were capable of. They would certainly make short work of her cubs. The hair round her throat bristled. She drew her lips back to show the size of her incisors and snarled again.

The leader of the pack sat apart from the others and stared at her. Its head and shoulders were red with blood. The other dogs were looking at her now and she saw the body of an antelope under their feet. They began to howl at her and mill around.

The antelope's blood smelt very fresh. Sabba thought the dogs must have killed it in the last twenty minutes or so. In that case there might just be a chance.

The dogs were uncertain what the lion wanted unless it was to try and take their kill from them. They looked to the leader who was already gorged with meat. Sabba's eyes never left his face. The dog stretched itself then casually began to scratch. With a greedy murmur of approval, the rest of the pack bent their heads and tore at the carcass again.

Sabba, not relaxing her snarl for a moment, growled at the cubs to follow her. Sure-footedly, she climbed up out of the gully. The cubs scrambled after her though not before Kitu slipped several times. As soon as they were all out, she set off at a fast pace to get as far away as possible before the dogs finished eating. The cubs struggled after her.

The sun was well up by now and Kimba was starting to pant. Sabba did not spare them. She kept stopping to look back in case the dogs were coming after them. As the cubs caught up with her she started off again.

The grass was higher here and thicker. It came up

to Kimba's shoulders, slowing him down still further. The flies had found them and a small cloud followed him, buzzing round his ears. Bad-temperedly, he swatted at them, slipped and rolled over. He lay full length on his back on the ground. His eyes closed. A wave of tiredness swept over him. It felt wonderful. He just wanted to lie here and sleep.

Then a shadow covered his face. It took a moment for it to register before he was up on his feet, wide awake and all senses tingling. He looked up into the face of the biggest lion he had ever seen.

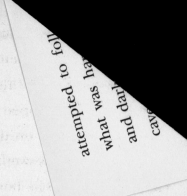

attempted to foll
what was ha
and dar
cave

Four

Black Mane grunted and opened his mouth very wide. Kimba had a jumbled impression of huge teeth, bristling whiskers and a long red tongue. Then he was running for his life.

He was vaguely aware of other lions all around him. Huge tawny shapes. Their smell was everywhere and he knew they were staring at him. Behind him there came a terrible roar. He had no idea where his mother or any of the other cubs were. He kept running. There was a thick bush some metres ahead and he dived headlong into it. He pushed and scrambled until he was deep inside, then lay down shaking.

At first, all he could hear was his heart pounding. Slowly, he got his breath back and the hammering sensation in his head began to ease. No one had

ow him in. He strained to hear
ppening but the bush was very dense
inside. It was rather like being back in the
again.

After a while, he sat up. Dust from the branches
got into his nostrils and he sneezed, loudly. Rigid
with horror he waited to be discovered. No animal he
knew could resist coming to investigate a sound like
that. But to his great surprise, nothing happened.

Time passed slowly. Kimba wondered if his enemies
were watching the bush and waiting for him to come
out instead. That's what he would have done. He knew
time was passing by the way the light became a little
brighter down here by the roots.

He wanted to cry out for Sabba to come and rescue
him but something inside always stopped him. In the
end, hunger and curiosity got the better of him and
he began worming his way through the undergrowth.
He kept behind cover and peered cautiously out
through the last layer of leaves. Nothing! He craned
his neck as far as he could but all he could see was
parched brown grass stretching away on all sides, as
far as the eye could see.

There was no sign of the huge lion or his mother.
He came out of the bush and stood there, blinking

in the harsh sunlight. He heard a faint rushing sound somewhere over his head. A shadow flicked over the ground in front of him and was gone. Startled, Kimba looked up. He saw a black speck falling out of the sky and more following.

Vultures! Another one swooped low over the top of him and he heard the rush of wind through its ragged feathers. It landed some distance away and clumsily hopped behind a group of rocks.

Kimba was intrigued. There must be a kill of some sort over there. Sabba had told them about vultures. All lions watched out for them. Whenever they appeared, it meant there was food nearby.

Kimba felt fresh pangs of hunger. He would be careful and just take a look. Perhaps he might even find Sabba and the others there. The thought cheered him and he set off at a run.

More vultures were landing by the time he got to the rocks. He was cautious now, careful to look all around him and stopping to listen. He left the rocks behind and followed the sounds of the birds feeding. The ground fell away into a deep depression and he looked down at thirty or more vultures packed together round the body of an eland.

Their beaks were dripping red and they jostled

and fought for the best places to feed. There was another animal there as well. An ungainly-looking creature with a sloping back and a broad, heavy head. The hyena looked up at the lion cub in surprise. Then turned to snap at a vulture which had come too close. The bird hopped to one side, beating its wings in fury. Another vulture landed beside the hyena.

The eland had been old and riddled with tick disease. It had died shortly after the hyena had found it lying on its side in the grass. The hyena studied Kimba and wondered where the cub's mother could be. It looked round quickly. By now, the air was thick with vultures. The hyena was being steadily crowded off the dead antelope.

It looked from Kimba to the vultures and then back again. Its eyes glowed and it began to sidle towards the cub. Kimba took a step backwards, snarling at the hyena. Hyenas were common enough animals. He must have seen hundreds of them in the past. But then, they had always kept their distance, patiently waiting for the lions to finish feeding. This one was becoming threatening.

Kimba snarled again and retreated still further. He didn't dare take his eyes off the advancing animal.

The hyena would take that as a sign of fear and come for him.

Step by step the hyena followed. It came up over the lip of the depression and quickened its pace. It was thirty metres away and closing.

Kimba kept giving ground until he felt the rocks at his back. Now he was trapped. There was just not enough time to scramble to the top. The hyena would seize him before he had got halfway. He tried to roar. The hyena's jaws opened for the first time in anticipation and it began to trot.

There was nowhere to hide. Kimba crouched low and did his best to roar. The hyena was running directly at him, coming in for the kill. Kimba was petrified.

There was sudden movement and noise on the rocks overhead. Furious snarling and a large animal leaping over him with its claws extended. The hyena spun round with a yelp and ran. The strange lioness chased it for about forty metres then watched it go. A ragged group of vultures rose in protest and, just as quickly, subsided.

The lioness padded back to Kimba and examined him closely. To the cub, she smelt safe and strangely familiar. She smelt like Sabba and he knew she was from the pride. He rubbed the top of his head against her side in respect and gratitude. Her name was Pemba and she was the youngest lioness in the pride. She licked him and reassured him in the silent way animals do.

The lionesses had been searching for him. Sabba had gone back to feed the other cubs. Pemba had seen the vultures and had come to investigate. Kimba nestled in close to her warm body. He trotted by her side when she took him back with her.

The pride lay under the trees. There were three lionesses and seven other cubs, all of them older than Kimba and his sisters. Black Mane lay under his own tree some distance apart from the others. He opened an eye as Pemba went past and Kimba dodged under her legs to keep away from him. As they approached the others, two large six-month-old cubs ran out towards them. Kimba bared his teeth.

Sabba saw him and called to him. It was a low, soft call not unlike a moan. He raced towards her. Soon, he was rubbing his body against her legs and playfully butting her with his head. Then he remembered how hungry he was and demanded to suckle. Sabba lay down on her side and let him feed. Kitu appeared alongside him but was shouldered out of the way by a bigger cub Kimba had never seen before. Sabba didn't seem to mind but Kimba spat at him then went on feeding.

When they had finished, Sabba took Kimba to meet Meru, the matriarch of the pride. Kimba stood quite still while the old lioness greeted him. Afterwards, Sabba began to groom her. She licked Meru's throat and shoulders, the roughness of her tongue making Meru croon with pleasure.

Next, Kimba met Chem, who was the mother of the older cubs. She was Sabba's half-sister and ranked immediately below Sabba in the pride. One of her cubs broke off playing and came over to join them.

Kimba stood up in anticipation as he approached. After much hesitation, Kimba touched noses with the stranger, then sprang back. They did it again but for longer this time.

The bigger cub reached out a paw and tapped Kimba on the side of the head. It was a challenge. Kimba dropped to his haunches and swung his tail. Fleeting memories of the hyena came to him giving him a sudden surge of confidence.

The cub leapt at him. Kimba rolled on to his back and raked at the stranger's nose with all four feet. He snarled and hissed in mock anger. It was a good game which the stranger, Tofu, won in the end. He eventually got his jaws round Kimba's throat and dragged him to the ground. They touched noses once again, then trotted off to find their mothers.

Later that night when the moon had risen, the pride lay back to back like dogs and slept soundly.

Five

Kimba's curiosity was boundless. He was interested in everything around him. He watched the lionesses rolling in elephant or buffalo droppings before they went out hunting. Sabba told him why they did it and he copied them to see if he could lose his scent too.

He was fascinated by baboons but couldn't understand why they ate so many duoma nuts. He had watched them for hours at the river, climbing the palms and ripping open the fruit with their teeth. He had tried chewing a nut and spat it out in disgust.

He found the tiny skull of a shrew and this became his greatest treasure until one of the bigger cubs pounced and ran off with it. Kimba searched everywhere but then forgot about it when it was time for the flying ants to start swarming.

He watched the adult lions closely and was on good terms with them all. On several occasions, he had stalked a sleeping Black Mane and once almost bit his tail. Then his nerve failed and he raced back to his mother.

He was lucky that Sabba was so patient and such a good teacher. She took him with her whenever she left the pride, pleased with his alertness.

That morning, Wheen and Kitu had demanded to come with them. Sabba had been very tolerant but it was obvious that they were only really interested in playing. Kimba became impatient. He was quite a bit bigger than either of his sisters. He growled at them and nipped their ears until they ran back to complain to the other lionesses. Then he chased after Sabba and caught her up.

Sabba headed for the river. They waited in thick green undergrowth at a place where the river bank was high and steep. It dropped down to the water in a series of worn terraces. The river was a hundred metres wide at this point, red with mud and sluggish. It was full of sand banks and ridges of smooth red rock. A stork was preening itself on one of them.

Sabba stepped out into the sunlight. A troop of black and white colobus monkeys in the branches of a tree on the bank opposite saw her and began screaming. She went halfway down the river bank and stood watching the surface of the river. Kimba joined her. A log drifted towards them.

It was Kimba who noticed the cloud of butterflies. They had settled on a patch of wet sand at the water's edge and were busy drinking. He leapt down the bank after them and tried to catch them between his paws. They fluttered away in alarm and he splashed after them, jumping high into the air in excitement.

The log was suddenly much nearer as if a hidden current was taking it in towards the bank. Sabba coughed in warning and Kimba froze with one paw still held high in the air in front of him. She called again. This time there was real urgency in her voice. Kimba scrambled up the bank towards her. It was much harder going than he expected. The bank seemed steeper and the ground crumbled under his feet. Small pebbles rolled down into the river. Sabba growled encouragement and stood over him as he got to the top and pulled himself over. She licked him then made him sit beside her and watch the water.

The log floated lazily by. Fifty metres downstream, when Kimba was losing interest, there was a sudden swirl in the placid surface and, to his amazement, the log came to life. He watched in astonishment as the crocodile heaved itself on to a sand bank and moved forwards on bent little legs. It was as long as the sand bank itself and lay in the sun with the tip of its tail still in the river. It opened its jaws and lay there motionless. It was as long as the python Sabba had found sleeping amongst the rocks, a couple of nights ago. Kimba remembered the silent way the crocodile moved and sensed its strength. He stared at it with respect and revulsion.

Sabba walked on along the river and he followed, still looking back at the motionless crocodile. She stopped beside a large patch of dried blood. There were tracks in the dust and scuff marks leading to the river. She made sure Kimba saw where they came from and where they led to.

She turned away from the river and Kimba saw the tunnel the crocodile had forced through the undergrowth. There were splintered branches and upturned bushes. A hundred metres from the river, Sabba found the place where the kill had been made. The ground was torn and stained and the bushes all round flattened by a huge tail.

The prey had been a waterbuck. A male. Kimba

recognised the scent. Waterbuck were large antelopes with coarse, shaggy coats. This one had been
killed by a leopard. Sabba showed him its pug
marks in the dust. The leopard must have decided
to eat the buck right away. The crocodile had smelt
blood and come to investigate. There had been a
fight. There were pieces of skin everywhere. The
crocodile had won and chased the leopard away.
It had dragged the carcass back to the river. Sabba
showed him its footprints and Kimba remembered
the size of the crocodile on the sandbank and
shivered.

Later in the day, when it got too hot to move, the
lions lay down under a tree. The air was as dry as a
stick and the heat was intense. Even the flies were
resting.

Kimba dozed for about thirty minutes then woke
up. He sat up and looked around. A bird flew down
in front of him. It put its head to one side and
looked at him. Kimba bared his teeth and it flew
off chattering.

Sabba was still fast asleep and dreaming she was
chasing something. He watched her lips twitch and
her paws move. Slowly, very carefully he backed
away and ducked down behind a bush. He peered

at her through the leaves. She had not moved. Kimba turned away in delight. He headed back to the river and sank down behind cover to watch for crocodiles.

He didn't see any and grew bored. There was a flicker of movement beside him and he flipped over a small stone. He had never seen a scorpion before. Puzzled, Kimba watched it sidling round with its sting raised high over its back. He prodded it.

The sting flashed down and buried itself in the thick fur around his paw. The next instant, it struck again. Kimba backed away, startled. He decided to go and find the place where the waterbuck had been killed.

Leaving the river behind him, he disturbed a flock of guinea fowl lying motionless in the grass. He had almost trodden on them before they broke cover and fled. A few paces further on and the air was full of powerful, new scents. He knew he had come across these animals before but that was all he could remember. He began to follow.

There were several of them. He thought there were two adults and a number of young, though he couldn't quite decide how many as their tracks kept criss-crossing. He was sure they were not small antelopes. Although the length of their stride was short, their tracks showed they were far heavier than the usual gazelle.

He found fresh droppings and knew they were not far ahead. Kimba began to stalk them, keeping his head down and bracing his body for instant action. He moved very fast between pieces of cover, just as he had seen Sabba and the others do. There was a sudden squealing ahead of him and he ran for cover under a bush. There, crossing the open in front of him, were a family of warthogs arriving back at their burrow. Kimba's mouth watered. Now he remembered what they were and how good they had tasted.

The little pigs began to play and the adults turned to watch. Kimba crept nearer. The warthogs did not notice him. He came closer. Surely they must see him now or hear the pounding of his heart? He was in the open, still moving towards them and very close. He unsheathed his claws and then a wasp flew into his face.

He jerked his head away without thinking. There was a loud grunt and the little pigs disappeared into the burrow. The female screamed at them to hurry, and followed. She entered the burrow backwards so she would face any intruder. The old boar turned and confronted Kimba. He stood his ground defiantly, shaking his head from side to side and slashing at the air with his tusks.

Kimba was shaking with excitement. His eyes never left the boar. He could see the flies buzzing round the warthog's face and the mud caked on the long black bristles of its shoulders.

He ran forward another body length, challenging the warthog.

The boar stamped, snorted loudly and charged from ten metres away. Kimba saw little clouds of dust springing up at its feet yet, somehow, he felt totally detached. It was a sensation he had never had before.

The warthog came at him in what seemed to be a long, slow glide. Kimba waited until the boar was almost on top of him, then he was side-stepping and leaping across the animal's back, his teeth biting ineffectively at the hard, wrinkled skin.

The boar screamed in panic. It slipped and fell on its side, crushing Kimba against the rock-hard ground. Winded, Kimba just managed to pull his head out of the way of those razor-sharp tusks.

He scrambled back on his feet, tail swishing, staring

into the warthog's little red eyes. Kimba snarled and took a stride towards it. The boar snorted, scraped its hooves in anger, then suddenly looked over its shoulder.

Kimba followed its gaze, saw the bushes quiver and there was Sabba glaring at him. The pig squealed, pivoted round and raced for the burrow.

Sabba looked directly at Kimba and spat at him. Then she was bounding after the boar. A couple of seconds earlier and she would have caught it. Instead, she landed in a cloud of dust on top of the entrance just as the boar tumbled inside.

Snarling in frustration, she started to dig, sending showers of sand and pebbles out between her back legs. But the ground was rock hard and it would have taken hours to dig the warthogs out. She stopped, glared at Kimba and then hit him so hard on the side of the head that he staggered and almost fell over. He crouched submissively in front of her. Sabba bit him hard on the ear while he howled in pain. Then she let him go and ordered him to follow her. She took him back the way he had come from the river. There in the dust covering his tracks, were the pad marks of a fully grown leopard.

Six

Kimba lay out in the open with his chin resting on his paws. A cloud of flies hung round his eyes and nostrils. He had learnt long ago not to bother trying to brush them away. It only excited them and made them more persistent than ever.

He was almost three years old and maturing into a well-developed young lion with a deep chest and the beginnings of a mane showing along his neck.

He had adapted easily to life in the pride. For the first couple of months, he and the other cubs had played and fought and tussled together. They had chased each other up and down termite hills and clung to low tree branches defying the others to pull them down. They had fought over porcupine quills and pieces of bone.

At nights, they had stayed behind when the pride went hunting and hid quietly in the grass until Pemba returned to lead them to the kill. By the time they had got there, Black Mane and the lionesses had taken their share. What little was left belonged to the cubs.

When the rains had come last year, Kimba and the others had splashed in the puddles and rolled in the thick red mud, revelling in the new sensation.

When he was thirteen months old, Kimba had almost died. His permanent teeth had begun to push through and his mouth was very tender and bled continuously. He had run a fever and became very weak. Meru the old matriarch, had stayed near and protected him from predators.

He had enjoyed being a cub but now powerful instincts were rising in him. He was the only young male left in the pride. The others were both dead, one trampled underfoot by a buffalo, the other killed by a bite from a solitary, wandering lion. Black Mane had heard the cub's cries and had driven the other lion away. But by then it was too late. The stranger had bitten the cub through the lower spine, paralysing its back legs. It had died twenty minutes later.

Kimba had inherited Sabba's love of hunting and

was a quick and willing pupil. He looked across at her now, sensing her sudden change of mood. She was sitting bolt upright staring into the distance. Kimba knew the signs. The other lionesses, Chem and Pemba, had also been alerted. They got to their feet, stretched and went over to join her. Kimba did the same.

Two miles away, a small herd of hartebeest had appeared. There were just six of them, all young males in their prime. They were grazing quietly though clearly bothered by flies. Kimba watched their sickleshaped horns tossing to and fro. He sat very close to Sabba and learned from them all.

Chem thought that the pride should wait until evening and then stalk the herd. This made good sense as the bucks were more active in daylight. But Sabba disagreed. This was a herd of young males with no foals or feeding mothers to slow them down. They could be a long way outside the pride's territory by sunset.

There was also a large pack of hyenas in the area. The lions had listened to them whooping and calling last night. Hyenas would certainly attack if they found the herd. Besides, the pride was hungry. Even allowing for Black Mane's share, a couple of hartebeest would provide enough meat for every-one.

Meru agreed with her and for the next ten minutes, the lions watched the direction the hartebeest were taking. They studied the ground in front of the herd, looking for good places to attack from.

Pemba was sent on ahead of the others. She was the fastest and her role would be to work her way round to the far side of the herd. The others would meanwhile fan out and approach the herd from the near side. Pemba would show herself and panic the hartebeest towards the waiting lions. It was a ruse they had used a hundred times and it worked more often than not.

Pemba moved off at a trot. The colour of her coat blended perfectly with the dried grass. However, like all lions, the backs of her ears were black and conspicuous over long distances. This helped lions keep track of one another while hunting.

They followed her progress while Pemba used the long tangles of thorn bushes and the ant hills as cover. They waited until she was finally out of sight, then left in single file.

Kimba learnt that hartebeest were easy enough prey to catch just as long as a lion got close enough.

Ten body lengths was the ideal distance to charge them from, Meru told him. Surprise was everything, as the lionesses never stopped reminding him. While lions can run at thirty miles an hour or more and accelerate very quickly, they can rarely keep up these speeds for more than hundred and fifty metres. On the open plains, most of their prey could outrun them. Meru had never forgotten how once as a young lioness, she had been outpaced by a warthog. The warthog had seen her a hundred metres away and had still beaten her to the safety of its burrow, sixty metres further on.

Kimba also knew that hartebeest, like most ante-lope, had good eyesight for noticing sudden move-ment. They were poor however at picking out motion-less objects. They were also colour blind.

The very first lesson Sabba had ever taught him had been to freeze the moment an antelope looked in his direction. She knew from experience that a motionless lion blends in perfectly with the ground and becomes almost impossible to see. That was why she could stalk to within ten metres of an antelope and still not be spotted.

The pride followed the herd at a steady walk. Half an hour later, they were two hundred metres away and in close country dotted with bushes. The lions sank down on their bellies and considered. There was no wind to worry about and the hartebeest continued to graze unsuspectingly. Kimba could hear them pulling at the grass and murmuring amongst themselves.

Meru and Sabba decided to come in closer before Pemba showed herself and began to panic the herd. Sabba moved forward. Ten metres to her left, Kimba did the same, keeping his head low and his entire body tensed for action.

The noise of grazing grew louder. Kimba came round the side of a bush and suddenly there in front of him were two hartebeest, feeding well ahead of the others. The nearer of the two looked up in alarm. Kimba froze. He didn't dare look round to see if Sabba was nearby. If the hartebeest took fright now it would be his fault entirely. They would all bolt and the pride would stay hungry. He remained motionless for the next two minutes. Then the antelope bent its head and began grazing again. Kimba waited for another minute until the bucks moved a little further on.

Quick as a flash, he ran forward a metre and sank behind a clump of tall grass. The other hartebeest looked up but continued to chew. As its head swung downwards, Kimba was already moving stealthily towards it. The smell of the animal filled his nostrils and his mouth began to water. He swallowed and crawled closer.

From a bush somewhere to his right, a bird chattered in alarm. Immediately, both hartebeest straightened up. One of them snorted and stamped.

Then Kimba heard it. A single loud grunt. Pemba's grunt!

There was a chorus of brays and the sound of hooves on hard ground. The next moment, there seemed to be hartebeest everywhere, stampeding directly towards him. Kimba leapt forward to meet them. They were barely twenty metres away and closing fast. The leading buck saw him and screamed. It spun round in a cloud of dust and raced off to one side.

The others panicked for a vital couple of seconds. Kimba saw their eyes bulging in fear as he raced in for the kill. Now there were hooves plunging at his head. There was dust and screaming and hartebeest bunching together, fighting to get away.

Kimba sprang and seized a buck round the muzzle, snapping its jaws shut and covering its nostrils. It reared up and swung the lion off his feet. Kimba hung on. The buck braced its front legs and tossed its head from side to side trying to break the suffocating grip. Frantically it sucked for air.

Kimba bit harder and dragged the buck's head back down. Sabba came racing up and he felt the buck stagger as she leapt for its throat. The hartebeest fell on its side. Kimba kept his grip and forced the buck's head backwards exposing more of the neck. Sabba found the windpipe and bit deep. A couple of minutes later, the buck gave a final convulsion and died. From nowhere, a vulture appeared and swung high above them in the bright blue sky.

They stood aside when Black Mane came and let him feed first. When he had finished, the lionesses rushed forward, Kimba with them for the first time. Chem snarled at him but he barged past her and started to feed. Behind them the new cubs complained, waited their turn.

When there was no more to eat, the pride walked to the river. They crouched down and drank, their long pink tongues lapping at the water like domestic cats.

It had been Kimba's first kill and that night he slept with his legs in the air, lying against Sabba in total contentment.

Seven

Meru was angry with Black Mane. She was also hungry. They all were. At this time of the year, game was always scarce. The rains were coming. It was hot and humid and the sky was grey and sullen. It pressed down on the plains like a huge, soggy blanket.

They had not eaten for four days. Almost all the resident animals who grazed across the pride's territory had been taken by lions, leopards or hyenas. It would be a different story in a couple of weeks when the vast herds of wildebeest arrived. But, until then, the pride had to survive as best they could.

However, last night, they had had a wonderful opportunity to make a big kill and Black Mane had let them down. At dusk, Sabba had found a small herd of buffalo feeding near the river. She had watched them intently. While there were no calves or obviously diseased animals amongst them, there was an old bull who might prove vulnerable. But to be sure of killing him, she and the other lionesses would need Black Mane's great strength and weight to pull it down.

She laid her plans while her stomach ached with hunger. They would wait in ambush by the river and attack the buffalo while they were drinking. She would go direct for the bull's throat and choke off the air supply. The other lionesses would attack from the side and bite through the tendons in the bull's back legs. Black Mane would then leap on its back and drag it to the ground.

But when she and Meru approached him, Black Mane had chased them away. He was bad-tempered. With his great thick mane, he was feeling the heat and the humidity far more than any of them.

But there was also something else worrying Meru. It was a good three days since Black Mane had last patrolled the pride's territory. He had roared last night to warn off intruders but that was not enough. This was the time of year when other prides and solitary lions tried to carve out new hunting grounds for themselves in anticipation of the arrival of the migratory herds. Soon, the plains below would be covered with tens of thousands of antelope and their foals. The pride would not go short of meat then for the next six months, unless they were driven out by rivals. Preserving the pride's territory was Black Mane's most important role.

Meru was sixteen years of age which is very old for a lion in the wild. She was also wise. She had known six previous dominant males before Black Mane. Lionesses were the only permanent members of a pride. Male lions led the pride until they were forced out in their turn by younger or stronger rivals. Black Mane was the largest male lion Meru had ever known. He had defended their territory single-handedly by virtue of his size. But he was lazy and jealous of any other male lion or cub. All the other dominant males she had known had accepted another male to help defend the pride but not Black Mane.

Soon Meru knew he would force Kimba out. Kimba was three now and almost mature. Black Mane had recently cuffed him savagely round the head and bitten his shoulder. If the younger lion had not flattened himself in submission, he would have been forced out then and there. Black Mane had stood over him, threatening to rip out his throat. Eventually, Kimba had escaped and crawled away on his belly.

Then at dawn today, they had heard other lions, strangers, roaring at Black Mane in defiance. He had replied half-heartedly and gone back to sleep. Meru sighed and slowly got to her feet. Her joints ached and she always seemed to be in pain these days. Soon the hyenas would catch up with her. But in the meantime . . .

She called the other lionesses to her and together they went and stood around Black Mane. Meru put her head back and roared at him. The others did the same.

Black Mane snarled but made no other protest. Besides, he was bored just lying here waiting for the rains to come. He stretched, ripping great furrows in the ground with his claws and strutted away. They watched him until he was lost to sight in jumbled rocks at the foot of a kopje. They stared at the plain, watching for any other signs of movement.

Black Mane did not have to go far before finding evidence of intruders. In thick undergrowth in a ravine behind M'goma Hill, he discovered that three different lions, all males, had been there during the past couple of nights.

He spent some time smelling the branches, memorising their scents. Then he backed into a bush and sprayed urine over it. He deliberately sprayed more over his own hind feet. This would leave an unmistakable trail across his territory and be a warning to all of them.

Three hundred metres further on he found a bruised leaf lying in the dust and a damaged branch above it. One of the intruders had left the narrow path and had climbed up the shoulder of the hill. Black Mane hesitated. He looked up the hill and saw the line the stranger had taken through the bushes. It was a very steep climb. Too steep for his liking. Instead, he was content to follow the greater threat from the two young males who had continued straight on.

He padded along silently, listening hard for any sign of them. It was thick bush along the ravine and it restricted visibility to only a couple of metres. It was very still as if everything was holding its breath. He came to the place where they had made a kill and grunted in anger. It had been an impala and most of the bones were now chewed clean. Jackals had been here since and would be hiding somewhere nearby now.

Black Mane examined the intruders' paw marks and began to form more of an impression of the two lions. There was no mistaking their hostility. They had sprayed their defiance liberally over the bushes on either side of the track. It was a direct challenge to him. Black Mane gave a full-blooded roar and walked on snarling.

He crossed and criss-crossed his territory throughout the following day and night looking for them. In human terms, it was an area measuring about fifteen square kilometres and Black Mane knew every bit of it. He knew where the best shade was to be found and the best places to watch from. He knew which river crossings the herds preferred. He knew the places to avoid for tsetse fly and where the borders with other pride's territories lay. The thought of others challenging him for it enraged him. He was going to find them and rout them.

He was up on a ridge that separated his territory from another when he saw them. Two lions, quite young though bigger than Kimba. They were some way below him, squatting and obviously eating something. It had been the sudden movement of their heads while feeding that had caught his eye. Black Mane looked for the quickest way down. For a big male he moved fast.

He was standing ten metres away from them before

they realised he was there. His roar of anger took them totally by surprise. Black Mane roared again and walked towards them. They roared back and moved a couple of metres apart. But they stood erect and gave no sign of backing down.

Black Mane swung a huge paw at the lion to his right and tore a clump of hair from its mane. He hit it hard on the head with his other paw and saw it stagger. But the other lion was in behind him and Black Mane's spine was dangerously exposed. Black Mane spun round and slashed it across the face. Blood welled from its upper lip.

The other lion came in at a run and Black Mane only just had time to half turn and aim a bite at it. He charged at the two of them and chased them back almost twenty metres. Then they separated and Black Mane saw he was vulnerable again.

He was more cautious now. Although they were young, he knew they were dangerous opponents. They worked well together; one trying to distract him from the front while the other went in for the killing bite in the middle of the back.

There was a great deal of snarling and many more threats before the intruders finally backed away. They ran off into the bush and Black Mane listened until he could hear them no more. He knew they would be back.

He looked to see what it was they had been eating. It was an old porcupine and they had eaten most of it. The hunger gnawing away inside him suddenly became unbearable. He lashed out at the dead porcupine, meaning to knock it out of the way. Instead, there was an agonising stab of pain and he was gazing at a paw full of broken quills and blood welling up around them.

It was mid-morning by the time he hobbled back to the pride. They saw there was something wrong from a long way off and ran to him. The sky was black with thunder and the light was fading by the minute. A cold breeze began to blow.

They looked at his wounded paw and rubbed their heads against him in sympathy and concern. There was a dazzling flash of lightning and the sky seemed to crack in half. It began to rain. Rain that bounced back up from the ground at head height. Rain that stopped them in their tracks.

They stood huddled together around Black Mane, their eyes closed against the rain and knowing that when it stopped, the pride would be open to whichever challenger got there first.

Eight

It rained steadily for the next eight days and afterwards the plains were covered with sweet-tasting grass. The river ran swollen and overflowed its banks. The crocodiles braced themselves against the current while they selected their victims from the herds of wildebeest and zebra that had still to cross.

For the lions, it was a time of plenty. The pride sat together on a low hill watching the families of zebra spread across the plain as far as the eye could see.

It was early evening. Soon the pride would move out and begin the night's hunting. First though, there were the rituals to be observed: habits that bonded them even closer together. Every day at about this time, they groomed and formally greeted one another. The cubs first approached Pemba, the youngest lioness, and rubbed heads with her. Next they went to Chem, then Sabba and, finally, Meru. The lionesses then did the same with one another, Pemba going first. Kimba, although a mature male, was part of the hunting party and was included too.

Black Mane, as always, remained aloof from it all. He had the automatic right to eat the lion's share of whatever animal they brought down. His appetite was immense. He could eat up to fifty pounds of meat at one time. He had also been known to refuse to share a carcass with any of the lionesses.

But tonight was not like old times. Black Mane was close to starving. The lionesses had tried to keep the hyenas away from their kills but by the time Black Mane limped there, there was very little meat left for him.

In despair he had tugged and pulled at the porcupine quills and got most of them out. Unfortunately, two of them had broken off inside the paw itself. The wounds had turned septic and now the poison was slowly spreading up Black Mane's leg. He could not bear to put any weight on the paw. The sound of his painful roaring may have been dulled by the rain but it had still been heard by many animals. He snarled after the lionesses and

Kimba as they left and went back to licking his paw.

Sabba led them at a slow walk through dense new undergrowth. She intended to ambush a family of zebra. The best time for this she knew was after they had finished drinking. Then they would be bloated and heavy and more likely to be off guard.

Zebras liked to drink at sunset in contrast to wildebeest which preferred the dawn. Sabba knew how long it should take to reach the river and did not want to get there too soon and risk being discovered.

The pride walked steadily on. Sabba stopped a number of times to raise her head above the grass and look round. When they were four hundred metres from the river she found what she had been looking for. A family of twelve zebra were milling about close to the river bank. The stallion was keeping guard while the mothers and their foals took it in turns to drink and play.

The lions stopped and stared at them. Kimba remembered Sabba's warnings. Zebra were difficult animals to bring down and far more likely to escape than wildebeest. They had powerful, razor-edged hooves and, unlike antelopes, they used their back legs as a weapon to lash out with. A badly-timed attack or a lucky kick could mean a broken jaw or a fractured leg. Both were equally fatal for a lion.

Zebras would never knowingly allow a lion to get within eighty metres of themselves. That was the animal's safety margin from attack. There was not a lion living who could catch a healthy zebra, given such a start. Lions like all cats had poor stamina and a fast chase over three hundred metres usually left them panting.

Sabba's plan was simple. She showed Kimba where to wait and walked on with the others. Kimba watched her intently. He could just see the black tips of her ears moving through the grass. She raised her head and looked back at him. He saw her snarl.

Obediently, Kimba stood up in full view and ambled forward. The zebra stallion brayed in surprise and all heads turned to watch the lion. Kimba knew that Pemba and Chem would now be fanning out twenty metres on either side of Sabba. Meru was some fifty metres behind Sabba, ready to support either flank if needed.

Kimba walked casually across the front of the zebras some hundred metres away. When he came opposite the stallion, he put his head back and roared. He then turned towards the stallion and began to walk towards the herd. He broke into a trot.

The younger zebras were becoming uneasy and started to bunch together. This distracted the stallion who kept looking round at them. Kimba came twenty metres closer.

The stallion looked at the approaching lion, then back at the river. He brayed and pawed at the ground in indecision and wondered if there were other lions hiding nearby. He had survived for six years on the plains and knew that the really dangerous lions were the ones that did not show themselves.

Kimba kept walking. He was now well inside the zebra's safety distance and the stallion was growing increasingly agitated. The other zebras were tossing their heads and skittering to and fro. The females were calling their foals close to them.

Fifty metres out, Kimba charged straight at them and the zebra were off and running. Crouched in the grass, Sabba chose her prey, a plump, young female with a foal running beside. As the herd came pounding towards her, Sabba timed her run. As the zebra galloped past, Sabba was racing alongside and leaping at full stretch for its back. Her claws sank into the animal's neck and rump.

The zebra screamed in panic, looked for its foal and tripped. It went sliding down with one leg thrust in front of it. Chem leapt over Sabba and seized the zebra by the neck. She dragged it over and on to the ground.

Sabba bit deep into its throat and held on until the convulsions finally stopped. The lions got up and looked around. Pemba and Kimba had also been successful. They dragged the dead zebras by the shoulder twenty metres towards some bushes. The carcasses were heavy and when they had done it, the lions were tired. By then, the zebra's eyes were glazing over.

Meru roared for Black Mane to come then joined the others and began to feed. Black Mane heard her and grunted in reply. He began to limp down the hill to join them. The ground was covered with sharp edged stones and he could not avoid stubbing his injured paw against them. Only hunger drove him on.

He sensed the presence of the intruders long before he heard them running across the plain. He stopped and snarled into the darkness. And then they were staring at him, a couple of body lengths away. He knew who they were and why they had come. For some minutes the three male lions stood motionless with bared teeth and ears flat against the sides of their heads.

The intruders grew in confidence. Cutlip, the dominant one, lunged suddenly at Black Mane. It was a quick, provocative movement and it showed Cutlip just how lame and helpless Black Mane had become. He moved closer and roared in triumph and thrust his jaws close to Black Mane's head. Tula, the other intruder strutted round behind Black Mane. It was the walk of an executioner. Nothing could be clearer.

Cutlip roared again and cuffed Black Mane with his claws extended. Black Mane took the blow, snarled and struck back. But his weight was on the injured paw and he staggered and fell on one knee. Behind him, Tula roared and raked him with his claws.

Black Mane rolled over on to his back in submission. They cuffed him and bit at his head but let him go. They watched him limp away. Then they went in search of the rest of the pride.

They soon found the smell of fresh blood on the warm night air and heard the pride eating. The two newcomers burst in amongst the feeding lionesses, scattering them in panic. Sabba was bowled over but it was Kimba that Cutlip was looking for.

Kimba slashed him along the flank but the other male was on him in a flash. Claws ripped at Kimba's head and eyes. There was a crushing weight on his shoulders. Kimba fell but twisted sharply to one side as he did so, throwing the other off balance. He landed on top of the intruder and bit down hard at his shoulder. He heard it give a grunt of pain then Kimba was running for his life towards the river.

Cutlip roared in triumph and planted both feet on the body of one of the dead zebras. He roared again. The lionesses huddled together, dazed by what was happening.

One of Pemba's cubs made a sudden rush for the carcass. It began to tear at it, greedy to eat. Cutlip bent down, took it by the neck and tossed the cub high into the air. Then he bit it through the backbone.

He roared again. The pride and their territory were now his.

Nine

Cutlip and his companion roared all night long. The sound of their roars followed Black Mane's retreating figure. As the dawn broke, Cutlip stopped to feed and afterwards they slept.

The grey morning light revealed the totality of Black Mane's defeat. He was now a stumbling figure that needed to stop and rest every hundred metres against an ant hill or a bush. The antelope herds watched him approach and parted to let him limp through. They stood looking after him, chewing contentedly.

A pair of crows spotted him and followed. When they realised how distressed he was, they landed and hopped along beside him, their beady eyes glistening with malice. The crows jeered and jumped back into the air and flew round his head. They swooped low, looking for a chance to peck at his eyes but his roar frightened them off and in the end, they flew away.

Black Mane pressed on, trying to put as much distance as possible between Cutlip and himself. Besides, there were far worse things than crows to worry about. Hyenas, for one. He knew he must find a place to hide, a cave or dense thicket where his enemies could not take him by surprise. When he finally reached water, he was almost too weak to drink. He collapsed on the ground beside the stream with his eyes closed in exhaustion.

Slowly, the sand under his chin filled with water. He gave a tentative lap then another and inched forward until it covered his paws.

He lay like this for a long time, dozing on and off while the fever in him grew. He groaned out loud and his mind slipped back to the time when Meru had been so ill not long before the birth of their first cubs. She had taken him to a special place and eaten the grasses there. He had gone with her and stayed near until she was healthy once again.

As night fell, Black Mane's head began to pound. The pain was so intense it drove everything else from his mind. He stared up at the stars and slowly focused his gaze on one part of the sky. Somehow he staggered to his feet. He walked in a dream as the fever raged, unaware of shapes that appeared and stared at him, of animals calling to each other and the cries and screams of the night.

He went on past M'goma Hill and up into the high country beyond, stumbling along in a daze. This had once been the furthest extent of his territory. He was not aware how marshy the ground was becoming until his legs finally gave out and he fell into a clump of bright green ferns. There were orchids everywhere and moss growing on the branches of the trees. He began to chew the tips of the ferns. They had a yeasty taste.

That night, while he lay close to death, the fever broke inside him. He woke, knowing the worst was over. His body was already rejecting the broken quills. A day later, he pulled the last splinter from his paw and knew real happiness.

The pad was still tender but at least he could start to walk on it again. A mist hung in the air as he left the place and he was glad to reach the river and feel the warmth of the sun again.

The paw hardened and soon he found he could

run for short distances. While he was doing this, a wild pig blundered into his path. Black Mane killed it with a hard cuff to the head. He ate it then and there, leaving only its feet for the scavengers. Nothing he had ever eaten had tasted so good. Strength began to flow in him and with it self-confidence. He found a place to lie up on the river bank and he was lucky again later that evening.

An impala stooped to drink at the river's edge and Black Mane seized it as it turned away. He dragged it back to his hide and spent the rest of the night eating it. When he had finished, he felt almost like his old self. He started to groom himself. Then he heard Cutlip roaring in the distance and his good mood deserted him.

Black Mane listened hard. Cutlip and his companion were some distance away, he decided, three or four kilometres perhaps. They were the only ones in the pride who were roaring. What had happened to Meru and the others? There was no sound at all from the females. Had they left? He growled at the thought.

The roaring grew louder. Cutlip and the other lion were confident and certain of their strength. Their voices warned what they would do to any lion they found on their territory.

As he listened, Black Mane thought he heard a roar of defiance from another lion. It was a long way away. Too far for him to be certain of its exact direction. Cutlip must have heard it too. He became angry and roared back even louder.

Black Mane's mouth opened to hurl his own defiance, then he remembered what it meant to face two opponents on his own and kept silent. The next time they all met he knew there would be no mercy shown and no submission. It would be a fight to the death. And to have any chance of winning, Black Mane needed to make an alliance with another male. But who?

And then he remembered. Kimba! Of course! Kimba. He must find him. Time was very important. Cutlip must not be allowed to settle while Black Mane still held two important advantages.

He knew the territory well and with Kimba there to help him, he had surprise on his side. As long as Cutlip thought he had been eliminated as an opponent, Black Mane could choose the time and place for the final showdown. He grunted, pleased with himself. If Kimba was alive he would find him. And if he was dead too . . .

It had not been a good time for Sabba. For a start, Meru was ill. All day she had lain on her side, barely moving. When Sabba had gone to her she had made no effort to greet her. Instead, Meru had closed her eyes and panted weakly. Sabba licked her head and neck then went to sit on her own in the shade. The lionesses were upset and irritable with one another. Sabba was in cub once again and would soon be leaving the pride to have them.

She had seen Cutlip kill Pemba's oldest cub and knew that any male cub of hers would face the same fate. Pemba seemed to have forgotten about it or was perhaps too frightened to protest. Instead, she busied herself looking after her three remaining cubs.

Chem was starting to flirt with Cutlip. Her own cubs were both female and would soon be mature. She wanted them to stay with the pride and breed. Sabba knew that Chem would soon start to roar with the new males. Pemba, being the most submissive, would join her. If Meru died, as seemed likely, then Chem would become the dominant female while Sabba was away having her cubs.

Sabba knew that she would either have to accept this or face being driven away on her return to the pride with the cubs. Chem and Sabba had already had one fierce spat which ended with Sabba ripping Chem's ear with her claws. Cutlip and the other male had both seen Chem's humiliation.

With this tension building inside the pride, it was not surprising that the hunting had been so bad. Last night, they had missed two wildebeest and had to make do with an emaciated gembok that was dying of disease. Cutlip was angry and very hungry and had chased the lionesses off the kill.

Later, he had snarled at Sabba and nipped Kitu as a warning which Sabba understood only too well. The future looked grim for her and her remaining cubs. She guessed she would never see Kimba again and Black Mane must certainly be dead by now. If she could not accept the new order within the pride, then she faced the miserable prospect of bringing up her new cubs out on the plains on her own.

It was a silent, miserable Sabba who eventually fell asleep in the rain later that night.

Ten

Meanwhile, Kimba lay in dark shadow under a rock, listening to the baboons screaming at each other. There were two rival troops, each trying to oust the other for control of the valley below.

It was country Kimba had never been in before and he had come here almost starving and in despair. It was far to the west of his old pride's territory. He had seen the range of mountains on the horizon and decided it would be easier to find food amongst the rocks and gorges than out on the plains. It was leopard country and he had found fresh markings on the rocks when he got here the night before.

He was more hungry than he could ever remember. Hunting on his own, he had soon found, was difficult and quite different from what he had been used to.

He had found it almost impossible to get within striking distance of a zebra or wildebeest without being seen by one of the herd and the alarm raised.

Many times over the last two months, he had lain perfectly still waiting for the herds to grow forgetful and come within range. But it had never happened. Recently, a large group of two hundred or more zebra had approached the patch of grass he was lying in. But a hundred metres from him, they had separated and passed by on either side.

Kimba knew that he had no chance of outrunning any of them over that distance. To make it worse, the herd had stopped and faced inwards, watching him. Shamefaced, he had pretended he had been asleep and walked away as casually as he could.

During all this time, he had kept well away from the river, reasoning that it was the most likely place to meet Cutlip and the other lion. He had listened to them roar and enjoyed hearing their anger when he roared back.

He thought of Sabba a great deal and wondered if Black Mane was dead. Since he had last seen them, he had walked across territory belonging to several other prides and had been challenged only once.

Hunger and isolation were making Kimba a fiercer

and more formidable animal. Although he had agreed to move on when confronted by the two resident males, he did so at his own pace. The other lions had followed quietly until he had left their territory.

It had taken him the last three nights to get here and he had not found much to eat during the walk. Only one hyena kill. He had heard them eating and had driven a small pack off a kudu bull. He had fed greedily until he heard other lions approaching. Outnumbered, he had slipped away into the night.

But now, the baboons were unaware of his arrival. In any case, it was unusual to find lions, even solitary ones, so far from the plains. All day, the rival groups screamed and postured and made forays into the other's territory.

They were powerfully built animals with close-set eyes under a protruding ridge of bone. They had long pointed muzzles like a dog and large, sharp canine teeth. They were intelligent, fierce and made excellent eating.

Kimba edged forward for a better view and spent the next hour engrossed. The two troops were evenly matched with a dozen or so highly aggressive males facing each other. The males made violent threats and gesticulated. They bared their teeth and screamed.

They were greatly outnumbered by the females, most of whom had babies clinging to their stomachs. The females, when not joining in the chorus of screams and hisses, were busy foraging.

Kimba noticed a couple of females moving away from the others and his interest quickened. They had their eyes on the ground looking for lizards or insects. Every now and then, one of them would stop and stuff something into its mouth. Then they continued to chatter and walk on.

There was a gully immediately below Kimba's hiding place. It was steep sided, full of rocks and stunted bushes. The two females now turned into it. One of them gave a shrill cry of delight. She put her baby down and started ripping the bark from a tree. The other female watched and made little whoops of encouragement. The tree was quite rotten and soon both baboons were reaching inside and pulling out handfuls of squirming, yellow grubs.

Something moved in the grass above them. Kimba's eyes widened. It was a fully grown leopard. Kimba had no idea how long it had been there and that worried him. He also remembered that baboons and dogs were a leopard's favourite food. The leopard glided silently down towards the baboons. One of the babies began to cry. Its mother bent towards it and stroked its head. The other female carefully licked her fingers, then looked up and saw the leopard poised above her.

She screamed. The baboons were in the open with the tree their only possible means of escape. She leapt towards it but was far too slow. The leopard caught her, shook her a couple of times and it was all over.

The other baboon snatched up her own baby and ran screaming back to the troop. The male baboons came at a run, swarming across the sides of the gully, whooping loudly. They stopped when they saw the leopard. The other baby began to scamper towards them. The leopard stretched out a leisurely paw and the baby lay motionless in the dust. The baboons howled in rage.

Kimba came out of cover. One of the baboons saw him and ran up and down in front of the others shrieking and pointing. The screaming intensified. The leopard looked round and saw Kimba bounding towards him. In one easy movement, the leopard took the baboon by the head and swung up into the tree. It raced to the very top fork in the branches and stood looking down, four metres above the ground.

Kimba roared in frustration and leapt for the tree.

He climbed quickly, driven on by hunger. The leopard watched him coming and its green eyes darkened. It knew it was safe at this height.

Kimba had not climbed a tree since he was a cub and then only to lie out along its broad, lower branches. But the smell of baboon was irresistible and Kimba clawed his way up until the old wood began to split underneath him.

The leopard was still a good metre above him when Kimba realised he could not get any higher. The branches would not bear his weight and he still had to claw the body away from the leopard. He hung on until his claws began to slip. Cat-like, he managed to turn round and came down the tree in a head-first slide and a shower of bark.

Something hit him hard on the nose. He shook his head in pain. There was a blow on his side and another. A piece of rock skidded across the ground in front of him. He sprang sideways and was hit on the leg. Safe in the rocks above his head, the baboons pelted him with stones. They were everywhere and he guessed both troops had joined forces against their common enemy. There must have been sixty or seventy of them, led by a number of old males who were directing operations. The noise was deafening.

More stones hurtled down and Kimba knew that one unlucky hit could lame him. If that happened he would be ripped to pieces.

He risked a glance over his shoulder and saw a wave of baboons closing in behind him. He roared and swung his head. Then he was running at them with all the strength he could muster. He jumped as high as he could and felt their hands and fingernails grasping at him. Kimba landed a few metres ahead of them and then outran them down the hillside. He did not stop until he reached open country.

He stopped to get his breath and listened to the baboons scolding and calling to each other for some while longer. Eventually, it became quiet.

It was much hotter down here and Kimba felt exhausted. He found a thick patch of undergrowth and pushed inside. He flopped down and was asleep almost at once.

The noise of cow bells woke him. He stirred, opened one eye and listened. It was a sound he had never heard before. Puzzled, he peered out. A long line of cattle plodded across the open plain half a kilometre away. They had their heads down and rolled from side to side as they walked. Calves followed at their heels. Four men and a number of small boys armed with sticks brought up the rear. They were laughing and talking amongst themselves. They were almost home. Soon it would be time for supper and for beer.

Kimba's interest quickened. He smelt the air very carefully. Then he became very still. He had never seen men before but he knew instinctively who they must be. He bared his lips in a snarl. Man was lion's greatest enemy. He caught their scent on the afternoon breeze. It was faint but unforgettable and unlike any other smell he had ever known. It was sweet and sickly and coated his tongue. It was the taste of death. He growled and felt the hair rising on his back.

The leading cow was thirsty. She could smell the water trough in the village and bellowed. The rest of the herd joined in and quickened their pace. The little boys ran alongside yelling happily.

Kimba watched their antics and listened to their thin cries. He was surprised how frail they looked. Like little pieces of stick, he thought. But he also remembered what Meru had told him and waited until the herdsmen had all gone past. Only then did he step out into the open and begin to follow them.

Eleven

Kimba peered through a screen of leaves and hardly dared draw breath. His heart thumped like a mad thing and his mouth was dry with excitement. The muscles in his legs trembled, bunched for instant flight. He stared wide-eyed at the noise and bustle of the village below, unsure of what to make of it. There were men everywhere. Men calling to one another. Men in groups. Some carrying their young on their backs. Men, sitting, standing, stooping. They looked so vulnerable. He could reach the nearest one in ten great leaping bounds and carry him off before any of them could stop him. And yet . . . instinct made him shiver and stay still.

Kimba watched a man chase after a dog. He had a stick in his hand and Kimba could hear the anger in his voice. The dog weaved in and out of the crowd of humans, sometimes even running through their legs. It easily outdistanced the man. The man threw the stick after the dog in rage and stopped to get his breath back. Kimba saw his chest heave. Later, the dog came back, sniffed at the stick and cocked a leg over it.

Kimba gave a low grunt of surprise and relaxed a fraction. He couldn't believe that men were so slow. If they couldn't even catch a dog! He eased forward for a better view.

It was a large village. Thirty huts were grouped around a low single-storied brick building. The building housed a medical centre and the office of the game warden for the local area. The huts were large and had round thatched roofs. Cooking fires were crackling and thin columns of wood smoke began to thicken. From the hillside above, Kimba watched intently.

There were pigs snuffling over a refuse pile and dogs tussling over scraps. A flock of goats picked its way daintily through the dust. Kimba's mouth watered as a hundred new scents rose towards him. There was a continual babble of voices and the yapping of many dogs.

He also noticed with increasing surprise that the men had no sentries posted. He looked carefully round the village again. But there was not a single human standing guard anywhere to warn of approaching danger.

He was amazed. These men were weak. They couldn't run fast. Even dogs weren't afraid of them. But for some reason, they appeared to be totally unafraid of anything. Even lions? Had Meru been wrong, or had she perhaps encountered a very different type of human? Kimba decided that that was the most likely answer. Whatever the reason, these men here were no threat to him.

He turned away and studied the cattle pen. It was on the other side of the village. Here again, Kimba could see no sign of any humans beings guarding it. The cattle were kept behind a stockade made of piled-up thorn bushes. In one place, the men had built a wooden fence with a wide gate in the middle of it.

As he watched, he saw a man come out, close the door behind him and drop a bar across it. Kimba's eyes gleamed. He would wait until the dogs had settled for the night and then go hunting. In the meantime, he stayed where he was, listening to the strange sounds the men made.

An owl watched him move silently down the hillside and pad across open ground towards the cattle pen. It blinked, hooted a warning and swooped into the night. Kimba heard the faint whisper of wind through its wing feathers but did not look up. All his concentration was centred on finding a way of getting inside the stockade. He had to eat. His hunger was now so intense it drove everything else from his mind.

He stopped by a lone tree and looked towards the village. He saw the huts and smelt the warmth of the animals sleeping there. He hesitated. It would be so easy. But he needed more meat than any pig or goat could provide.

The thorn bushes reached high over his head. Kimba stood up on his hind legs and teetered there while he measured the leap he would have to make to clear them.

He paused, sensing that there was another row of bushes behind and put there to snare predators like himself. Thorn bushes like this would deter every animal except a rhinoceros. And they were grass eaters. The men had been clever.

He skirted the fence studying its height. He examined the ground for any gullies he could use to worm his way in from underneath. Then he remembered seeing the man coming out.

The smell of cattle was overpowering. He quickened his pace and found the wooden fence. He stared up at it. Some of the cattle inside were becoming uneasy. They must have picked up his scent and were beginning to stir. He listened to them getting to their feet and heard the thud of a hoof stamping nervously. A calf made a low moaning sound.

Kimba drew back and considered. The gate was well over twelve feet high. The men had tried to weave long branches of thorn in and out of the gaps along the top. They stuck out at angles and Kimba knew they were no real obstacle.

The wooden wall was solid and stank of man. But if he could reach the top of it, it would be all too easy to slip down inside the pen. Any fear he might have had of humans had long since disappeared. Hunger was the only reality.

Kimba circled round a couple of times, silently measuring the jump he must make. He turned and came bounding in towards the gate, snarling his determination to succeed. He judged his leap perfectly. For a moment he hung spreadeagled with every claw digging deep into the wood. Then with a powerful thrust of his back legs he was balancing on top of it.

He felt the thorns slashing at his legs but ignored them. The cattle were staring up at him and starting to back away. He jumped down and they shrank in fear. They began to low in distress. Kimba walked towards them.

In the village, a dog awoke. It pricked up its ears and listened. Then it was wide awake and barking madly. Others heard and joined in, begging their humans to wake up and protect them. The men responded slowly, reluctant to leave their dreams. Besides, dogs were always barking at something. It was probably a family of elephants. There were a lot of them around.

By the time they realised their cattle were in distress, Kimba had seized a plump calf and was squatting down to feed. He ignored the men's shouts. His senses were reeling at the taste of the sweetest meat he had ever known. He ate greedily and felt strength flooding back through his veins. Behind him, the rest of the herd bellowed and pushed and struggled to get as far away from him as possible.

Kimba heard the men coming. Soon, strange lights flickered on the outside of the thorn hedge. There was an unpleasant burning smell that he didn't like. He growled and felt a tiny shiver of apprehension return.

He stood up, seized the calf by the shoulder and waited. A man's head showed suddenly over the top of the gate. Another appeared alongside. Then, several more. The men held flaring torches high above their heads. The light drove back the shadows surrounding the lion. There was a gleam of metal and something sharp and menacing thudded into the ground in front of him.

There were loud, stern voices shouting orders now. A dozen burning torches came twisting through the air towards him. Kimba roared and backed away. He saw the gate begin to swing slowly open. He watched and waited, his tail flicking from side to side. He roared again, warning the men what he would do to them. The air was full of the stink of burning oil. The gate was now half open.

Kimba bent down, took the calf in his jaws and walked towards it. At the entrance he stopped and roared again. It was hard to see. There were burning torches everywhere and he knew the men were hiding behind them.

He took a fresh grip on the calf and began to run

towards the darkness. He heard the men howling in anger behind him but by then he no longer cared. He stopped after a while to listen, but there were no sounds of pursuit. Satisfied, he lay down where he was and began to eat again.

Twelve

Kimba lay on his back in the sun. Life had never been so good. Not even when he was a cub. Then, there had always been older lions to be in awe of and bigger cubs snatching all the best things to eat. He gave a little sigh of contentment.

Last week, he had killed a fully grown cow and yesterday he had taken a young bull. He had never eaten forty pounds of meat at one sitting before. Reluctantly he had to leave what was left to the hyenas. He had stalked them both in the daytime, while they were out grazing with the rest of the herd. There was no longer any way now he could raid the cattle pen again.

The day after his attack, he had returned and watched the men erect a bristling new thorn hedge in front of the gate. At night, they put flaring torches in brackets on either side of it. Kimba had roared his defiance but after an hour had left to go hunting in the bush. But he could not forget how wonderful the calf had tasted nor how easy it had been to kill.

He had started to follow the herd to its grazing area each morning and spent all day observing it, watching for any stragglers. At first, the men were extremely watchful. They doubled the number of herdsmen and kept the cows close together. After four days, however, they relaxed and Kimba's patience was rewarded.

He stalked the cow into a patch of elephant grass and killed it with a single bite behind the neck. The cow had gone down without a sound. The men had not found out until it was time to return home and by then it was far too late.

Kimba yawned out loud and drowsily went back to sleep.

The headman and the village elders went to the game warden in despair. The meeting was a long one. The rest of the people stood on the veranda outside and listened in silence.

'You must shoot this lion,' the headman told the warden. 'Before he eats all our cattle.'

The warden shook his head and looked uncomfortable. 'It is not government policy to kill lion,' he told them. 'We are trying to preserve them. For the tourists,' he added, seeing the expressions on their faces.

'If you will not help, then we will kill it ourselves,' they warned.

The warden looked sceptical. 'You are not Masai and you do not have guns,' he told them rudely.

They considered this insult in silence. 'We have poison,' they reminded him after a long pause. 'Either you get rid of it or we will!'

The warden threw his hands in the air.

The telephone rang. The warden let it ring a dozen times, hoping that whoever it was would hang up. But they didn't. Feeling very cross, he picked up the receiver.

It was his counterpart from the neighbouring area. His message was brief and only added to the warden's problems.

'There's a band of poachers from over the border coming this way,' he told the elders as he slammed down the 'phone. 'They're shooting and trapping everything that moves.'

The headman shrugged. 'Why should that concern us?' he asked. 'The poachers only hunt wild animals and then sell their skins to the tourist markets on the coast.'

The warden banged a fist on his desk. 'They use snares don't they? And snares don't worry whether they catch cows or impala!'

'If this lion goes on living, we soon won't have any cows left,' they rejoined. 'Maybe these snares will catch the lion too.'

The warden met their eyes and eventually nodded. 'I'll do what I can,' he promised.

'Two more days,' they warned. 'Then we put down poison.'

As they left the brick building, the villagers cheered and clapped and began to argue about which was the best poison to use.

Kimba woke suddenly and knew at once that he was being watched. His breathing remained unchanged and he deliberately did not open his eyes or give any sign of being awake.

He was intrigued. There wasn't an animal he could think of that would have the courage to come this close to a sleeping lion. He listened very carefully, determining exactly where the mysterious stranger could be standing.

A moment later, he rolled on to his feet, an out-raged, snarling lion with one large paw held in front of his face, claws extended, ready to strike. But his anger quickly died and his snarls faded into the afternoon sunlight. In front of him was the oldest and largest lion he had ever seen. In his prime he would have been even bigger than Black Mane.

The stranger limped towards him, the ribs and hip bones showing through his battered hide. He only had half a tail and most of the claws in his front paws were missing. Kimba stood quite still and let the newcomer approach. As he came level, Kimba dropped his head in submission. The old lion was no threat to him and, besides, he was dying of starvation and old age.

His name was Kio and he had once been the leader of a pride of forty lions that had dominated the plains for close on six years. All the land from the river to the foot of the mountains had been theirs. They had killed or driven out the leopards from M'goma Hill. No other lion had dared enter their territory unless it was to challenge Kio for leadership. And Kio had defeated every one of them.

Kimba stood back and let the old lion push past him into the shade of a tree. Slowly, stiffly, Kio lay down. Kimba followed and stood over him. The old lion's head drooped on to his chest. He told Kimba of the fights he had had as a young lion and the greatest battle of them all, when he had first challenged for the leadership of the pride. It had lasted on and off for three days before his rival had dragged himself away. Kimba looked at Kio. Those great teeth had all gone now. In their place there were just these flattened stumps, incapable of ever tearing open a zebra carcass again.

Kimba shivered and knew it would be the same for him in the end.

Kio's face and nose were criss-crossed with old scars. There was a deep gash across his forehead and a hollow in his side where a buffalo horn had gored him. The only prey he would ever hunt when he was leader of the pride, he told Kimba, was buffalo. Nothing else was worthy of a lion. Not even elephants. Kimba stared at the tatters that were all that was left of his mane.

Buffalo, Kio told him, were the most cunning and dangerous animals of all. They could outrun any lion. They could spin round in a second and slash open any animal on the plains with one twist of their horns. Only man was more dangerous.

Buffalo's colouring made them almost impossible

to see at night or in deep cover. Kio had been attacked by them and chased up trees while the herd milled around below, waiting to trample him to death. Above all, it was their cunning that made them so dangerous to hunt.

Kimba looked up and to his surprise saw three spotted hyenas standing, watching them. For a moment he couldn't think what they were doing here. There was no kill to scavenge. They were less than ten metres away and behaving as if it was perfectly normal to be so close. He growled at them.

Hyenas were even bigger rivals than leopards. Many times, he remembered Sabba and the other lionesses being driven off a kill by a pack of these creatures. An adult hyena was quite capable of bringing down a zebra all on its own. It just lacked the single, great killing bite that all lions possessed.

One of the hyenas lay down and closed its eyes. Only then did Kimba realise why they were here. They were following Kio. They were watching him night and day, waiting for the moment when he would stumble or become distressed. Only his size still kept them at a distance.

Kimba's hatred exploded. Roaring in fury, he was halfway towards them before they realised what was happening. Panic-stricken, they scattered. Kimba caught one of them with a vicious cuff that sent it tumbling head-over-heels. He leapt after it and chased it through the undergrowth, raking his claws down its back. The hyena screamed but somehow still managed to squirm away. It plunged into a deep thicket of bamboo, howling at the top of its voice.

Kimba slewed round but there was no sign of the others. A hare suddenly shot across his path, terrified by the sudden appearance of the hyena. When it saw the lion, it froze in terror.

Kimba brought the hare back and dropped it in front of the old lion. It took Kio a long time to eat. Kimba waited patiently until every last scrap of fur or piece of bone had been swallowed.

Kio sighed and licked his paws. He slept for a while until the sun began to dip towards the hills. Then he got to his feet. The two lions stood facing each other.

Kimba looked into the old lion's eyes and suddenly wanted to be with his own kind again. He had given Kio food and in return the old lion had shown him where his future lay. Kimba knew then that he must return and win back his pride from Cutlip.

They rubbed heads and Kio turned away and did not look back. Kimba watched him walk towards the bush and then he was gone. Kimba put his head down and roared.

Later, just before the sun set, something made Kimba stop and look down on to the plain. It was Kio, walking slowly towards a stand of trees, his shadow lengthening in front of him. Ten metres behind, there were three other shadows stretching towards him.

Thirteen

Later that night, Kimba set off back to the river again. He came down the hillside for the last time. Out of habit, he circled the cattle pen. There was a lot of tension in the air. He could feel it quite clearly. The dogs in the village were wide awake and excited and the men were still moving around.

As he approached the wooden gate he saw why. A pack of hyenas was milling about underneath the solitary acacia tree. They were staring up into its branches. As he watched, one of them placed its front paws against the trunk and tried to scramble up.

Kimba walked over to have a closer look. To his surprise, he saw a dead goat wedged into a fork of the tree, about two metres above his head. It was in easy reach of a lion or a leopard. Kimba wasn't particularly hungry. He was still satisfied from the bull he had eaten. But this puzzled him. The hyenas slunk away to let him through, then closed in behind him.

He smelt the carcass very carefully. It was quite fresh, the blood still sweet smelling. And yet, there was something about it that Kimba did not trust. Goats had a strong natural odour. They were far more pungent smelling than dogs or even pigs. They also carried all sorts of other scents around with them, mainly on their feet and hocks. But this goat was clean and had very little smell. Kimba thought he could detect the very faint scent of Man around it. But he couldn't be sure. He remembered Kio's warning about man's cunning and decided not to eat it.

The hyenas were growing impatient. They began to whoop and cackle and run round in circles. Kimba knocked the goat out of the tree with a sharp blow of his paw. The hyenas fell on it, ripping at the soft flesh. They pushed and shoved past his legs, forcing him out of the way. For a moment, a strange, bitter scent wafted up from the goat's body cavity. Then it was gone.

He left the hyenas to it. Their shrieks and chuckles followed him for a long time. He left the men's village far behind and padded easily along a well-worn game path. There had been men along here too. He wrinkled his nose in distaste and began to walk more quickly.

The moon came out from behind a bank of cloud and flooded the ground with brilliance. He closed his eyes for a second against it and felt something very strong snatch at his left leg and yank it from under him. He fell heavily, slewing across the path. For a moment he lay there winded and shaken. Then he roared angrily and sat up to see what it was. Something very thin, like a creeper, was wrapped tightly around his shin. It gleamed in the moonlight. Furiously, he bit down at it, grinding it between his teeth.

But it was cold and inert and very strong and his teeth made no impression on it. Furiously, he bit at it again and again until his gums were bleeding. But no matter how hard he tried, he could not sever it.

He stopped biting and studied the thing more closely. He limped over and found where it had been coiled around a tree root. He threw himself backwards using all his weight to try and snap the wire. But the sudden pain was so intense he sobbed out loud. He was trapped. There was nothing he could do. This was Man's work. He was sure of it. A wave of panic swept through him. This time he attacked the tree root, slashing at it with his good paw, biting and savaging it.

But the root was very old and as hard as iron. After half an hour, Kimba gave up and roared his frustration and rage to an uncaring world.

Not long after sunrise, a swarm of biting tsetse flies found him. Hundreds of vicious, blood-sucking insects the size of small grasshoppers, settled on his back and flanks. The more he dodged and threw himself on the ground the more they came, attracted by the smell of his sweat.

He had a vivid memory as a cub of Sabba thrusting him into an old hyena burrow to escape them. Now, though, he was powerless to avoid their stinging agony. All that day they fed on him. When evening came, his body was covered with bare, blood-stained patches.

His tongue was swollen and sore. His mouth was full of dust. Swallowing was painful. As the night wore on, his thirst became worse. Towards dawn, a mist formed and he licked the leaves of the bushes on either side. He tried to reach as high as he could to get more. But what little moisture he found only coated his tongue with a gritty paste. And all the time, the wire mocked him and his helplessness. It was insignificant like a ribbon-snake. But it held him there against his will until Man should come and find him.

The sight of the wire gleaming in the early morning light sent Kimba mad with anger again. Ignoring the agony of his trapped leg he made a last desperate effort to break free. He crouched and sprang as high as he could into the air across the track. The root creaked and the wire cut deeper. But the snare held and Kimba turned a half-somersault and landed with a crash on his back.

He rolled over and tried to shake the thing to death. Bewildered and with his whole leg feeling on fire, his head fell back into the dust. He closed his eyes in misery.

The sun climbed higher and the ground began to bake. A solitary vulture swung lazily overhead but the biting flies did not come back. Kimba lay motionless.

Towards midday, he heard a strange noise like a swarm of bees approaching. It came nearer and nearer until he sat up and peered around.

He looked up at the sky but couldn't see anything in the glare. The noise was almost on top of him and he became alarmed. He saw a huge shadow racing over the ground towards him. It flashed over him and was gone by the time he got to his feet. He snarled after it. It must have heard him!

It came swooping back over him again but this time from the other direction. It did it once more, then seemed to lose interest. Its roar became a drone. Kimba followed its progress as it faded away into the great silence.

An hour later other visitors came: silent, dust-covered, grey ghosts. Kimba opened his eyes and looked up at the huge bulk of the elephant. Slowly, unsteadily, he scrambled up and found he was surrounded. There were two young bulls, five females, some with calves, and an old matriarch. Kimba's heart pounded. He tried to roar but barely managed a croak. Elephants and lions have little love of each other. Kimba had watched Sabba and the others chase and bring down a young elephant more than once. He knew he was in real danger of his life.

One of the females called her calf to her. It ran towards her and stood under her belly. Kimba bared his teeth and stared unblinkingly at the matriarch. The elephants shuffled closer. The old female arched her trunk over him, examining him. She lifted her right foot to knee height and let it fall. Kimba felt the thud and knew what she was going to do.

He crouched below her, teeth bared, pretending he was about to spring at her trunk. The elephant was not deceived for a moment. She could see Kimba's distress, his swollen leg and the way the lion tried to hide the snare under his body. She came very close until the lion was in her shadow. She looked down at him, measuring the distance, and slowly raised a massive foot.

As Kimba gathered himself to try and leap out of the way, two shots rang out in quick succession. Kimba had no idea what they were, but the effect on the elephants was electrifying.

The old female trumpeted in alarm. The huge foot slammed down just missing Kimba's head. He had a glimpse of folds of wrinkled grey skin then the air was full of dust and terror as the herd bolted round him.

Kimba heard men calling to one another. There was another flurry of shots but from further away this time. There were men close by. He could hear them running, their footsteps pounding across the rock-hard ground. Kimba felt real fear again.

A gazelle came leaping down the path towards him. It came to an abrupt stop when it saw him, then leapt sideways in a graceful arc and bounded off through the bushes.

The lion stood motionless for a very long time. Long after the birds had stopped their warning cries. He decided in the end that the men had been hunting elephants.

Relieved, he sank down and licked his leg. The wire had gone very deep and was hard to find. His skin and fur bulged over the top of it. He had long since lost any feeling in his foot. But the worst thing of all was his thirst.

During the afternoon, he began to slip in and out of consciousness. His breathing became shallow and laboured. It took him a long time to realise he could hear that sound again. It was the swarm of bees. It was coming back! He opened one eye and lay listening. He remembered the time he had found a bee's nest and his mouth was suddenly full of the taste of wild honey.

The noise grew louder until it seemed to be beside him. He opened both eyes and struggled to sit up. It was not bees. He had never seen a Land Rover before but he knew that man had finally come. He saw human faces staring out at him. He opened his mouth but no sound came. His head was going round and round. It was not easy to focus on the men. The wire held him tight. There was no escape.

He saw one of the men point a long stick at him and he knew it was a threat. But there was nothing he could do. He snarled defiantly. There was a loud bang. Kimba staggered in shock and bit angrily at the sudden pain in his side. He tottered on unsteady feet. Everything was going dark.

The men watched him slowly crumple and fall. 'Gotcha!' said the man with the gun.

Fourteen

'Give him five minutes just to make sure the dart's taken,' said the man with the gun. 'We don't want him waking up too soon, do we?'

'Poor old thing!' said the woman beside him. 'He really looks in a bad way.'

'Damn poachers!' exclaimed the man sitting in the back of the vehicle. 'Well, this is one skin they won't be getting.' He looked at his watch and picked up a radio handset. 'Vet One to Base,' he called a couple of times.

'Go ahead Vet One,' crackled the reply.

'OK Base . . . We've located the lion. We're just going to see how bad he is.'

'Roger Vet One! We're all ready for him.' The operator at the Wild Life Refuge took off his headphones and went outside. 'They've found that lion!' he shouted. There was a ragged cheer.

A few minutes later, the doors of the vehicle opened and the three people inside clambered out. The woman vet knelt down beside Kimba and carefully pulled back an eyelid. 'He's out cold,' she told them. 'We've got two hours to play with.'

One of the men prized open Kimba's jaws and the woman pulled his tongue out and placed it between his large incisors. Then they squatted down and examined the snare.

'Three strands,' said one of the men. 'Strong enough to hold a jumbo jet. Stand back!' he ordered and severed the cable with a pair of heavy duty wire cutters.

The wire sprang back. It quivered like a threatening snake, then lay still. They loosened the snare around Kimba's leg as carefully as they could. It took ten long minutes before it finally came away. The woman cleaned the wound. She gave Kimba a large dose of antibiotics and smeared ointment into the groove.

They backed the Land Rover up and filled buckets of water from a tank in the back. Then they poured them over the lions's head and body to counter heat exhaustion. They washed out his mouth and cleaned his tongue and gave him more injections. They took blood samples and poured still more water over him.

Finally, they held him by the shoulder and legs and rolled him on to a specially-designed trolley. They brought it to the tailboard of the vehicle and heaved and pushed and slid it inside.

Before they left, the men walked along the game path and found three more snares. They destroyed them and threw the pieces away. The sound of the Land Rover's horn called them back.

'Time to be going,' the woman told them. 'Unless you want our new friend here to take over the driving!'

Six days later, they decided that Kimba could return to the wild. Like all lions, he had amazing powers of recovery. The wound on his leg had healed cleanly and rapidly. His appetite was healthy and his deafening roars drowned out all conversation around the reinforced pen they kept him in. The woman checked first with the game warden who begged her to release the lion as far away as possible.

'The warden says those poachers are still in the neighbourhood,' she told the others.

'He's going to be real thirsty after you dart him again,' said one of the men.

The other man shrugged. 'So let's play it safe. Why don't we take him to the river, out M'goma way, and let him go there?'

'It's a long drive,' the woman objected.

'Only an hour,' he reassured her. 'And he'll be safe there.'

And they agreed.

Kimba opened his eyes and quickly closed them again. His head ached and his mouth was dry. He wanted to go on sleeping but the scent of humans in his fur and nostrils forced him to get up. He badly needed to drink.

A parrot saw him and screamed a warning. It flew up to the top of a tree. It put its head on one side and watched him passing underneath.

The smell of the river grew stronger. Kimba could see the tops of the tall palm trees along its banks. He could hear monkeys chattering and crashing through the branches. Two warthogs burst out of the bush and raced across the open ground to his left. They ran with their tails pointing straight up like car aerials. Kimba grunted in annoyance. He hadn't heard them coming. He must still be half asleep.

The river was cool and soothing. He sat on his haunches and drank for a long time, closing his eyes at the sheer delight of it all.

A log drifting in mid stream started to swing. A faint ripple showed on the placid surface. Then a warthog snorted from close by and Kimba was alert. And only just in time! He saw the grey tip of the crocodile's snout coming for him. It was barely a body's length away. For a fleeting second he was looking into the creature's eyes and saw the sudden gleam there. He knew it was judging the distance between the two of them and leapt backwards. He fled up the bank to safety.

The crocodile came out of the water at a run. It was almost six metres long and had lived in the river for fifty-nine years. Its name was Kirek.

It checked and watched Kimba leap into the bushes high above its jaws. Then it turned round and ponderously sank back into the river again. The monkeys stopped screaming and water seeped into Kirek's footprints. Life returned to normal.

Sabba did not go back to M'goma Hill to have her next litter of cubs. She found a family of leopards had been there recently. Their scent was still strong.

Pieces of bone littered the floor where the female had brought her prey back to eat. Sabba examined the rocks above and found the male leopard's favourite watching place. Instead, she chose a dense thicket near the river to have them. It was safe and she didn't have to go very far to find either food or water. At night or in the dawn, she hid beside the ant hills, waiting for an antelope or warthog to come down and drink. She could usually stay within a couple of hundred metres of the den and keep a constant watching eye on it.

Her four new cubs grew rapidly. They were all female, which reassured her. She was certain that Cutlip and Tula, the other new male, would not hurt them even though they were Black Mane's offspring. All females were vital future breeding stock for the pride.

The day after Kimba was returned to the river, Sabba set out with her cubs to rejoin the pride. She gave them a final lick and grunted for them to follow. She led them towards the hill where she knew the others had been the night before. The males had roared for the entire hour before dawn. The cubs followed, happy to be together and intrigued by everything around them.

After an hour, Sabba stopped. She had seen movement on the high ground ahead of her. There were lions coming down towards her. She called her cubs to her and studied the approaching animals very carefully. She recognised Pemba in the front and purred in delight. She roared a greeting. The two big males were some way behind and walking slowly. She wondered where Meru was and looked again.

There was no sign of Meru. Sabba scanned the crest line behind Cutlip, hoping to see the old lioness appear. She stopped purring. Sadly, she realised that Meru must have died. If Meru was dead, then she, Sabba, would be taking the old lioness's place. She roared another friendly greeting.

She saw Chem running towards her and was surprised. The sight of Chem reminded her that there might still be trouble ahead. Chem's cubs bounded after their mother. They had grown a great deal since Sabba had been away. They looked large and strong.

Sabba went to greet them. She thought she heard Pemba roaring in reply but could not be sure. All her attention was fixed now on the rapidly approaching Chem. Sabba realised suddenly that Chem was not coming to greet her at all. The reverse in fact. There was no trace of welcome on her face at all.

Sabba grunted at the cubs to remain still. Chem came bounding in towards them, snarling her displeasure. She stopped five metres in front of Sabba. Every line of her body showed aggression. Chem crouched in front of them, her face tensed in a fixed snarl. As Sabba watched she opened her jaws wide and roared. Sabba threw a quick glance at the cubs. They were sitting down looking about them and quite unaware of what was happening only a few metres away.

Sabba turned to face Chem and bared her teeth. The rest of the pride was approaching fast but Sabba's eyes never left Chem's face. Chem's tail was flicking from side to side. Her eyes were like slits. Sabba saw her take a deep breath and the next instant Sabba was rolling over on her back neatly avoiding Chem's attack and raking her claws along Chem's belly.

Chem landed on top of the cubs and they screamed in shock. Sabba leapt to defend them and slashed at Chem's legs. Chem twisted round and went for Sabba's throat. They swayed and struggled, hitting at each other and growling in fury. Then, as if by common consent, they separated and Cutlip moved between the two of them, roaring at them both.

Sabba ran to her cubs, shaking at the unexpected

ferocity of the attack. She licked and nuzzled them, reassuring them that it was safe. One of the cubs was whimpering and dragging itself awkwardly through the grass. Chem had trodden on it as she had landed.

Sabba had no time to give it any more attention when she saw Cutlip stalking towards her. He was half as big again as Sabba and had clearly become very dominant while she had been away.

Sabba saw Pemba standing nearby looking unhappy. Tula, the other male, was coming up to join Cutlip. Chem rubbed her head along Cutlip's flank and then went to meet Tula.

Sabba looked down at her cubs and knew she had no choice. Chem had become all-powerful. She crouched down in front of Cutlip and stayed motionless while he strutted past and examined the cubs. The big male grunted over them a couple of times and smelt them carefully. But he seemed to accept them for now. He came and stood beside Sabba.

His shadow lay in front of her and she did not dare move. Cutlip scratched at the ground and the dust flew into her face. He roared and without bothering to look at her, walked away.

It was time for the pride to move on. Sabba let Chem lead, grateful that she and her cubs had survived.

Pemba greeted her shyly and followed on behind. The cubs squeaked with excitement, glad to be on the move again. They chased each other around ant hills or clumps of grass. The injured cub kept up for the first hundred metres then had to rest because of the pain in her side. Pemba stopped to lick her then continued. The two males ignored it.

The cub fell further behind. It tried to run after the others at first. When that became impossible, it sat and wailed at their departing backs. Eventually it lay down, its broken ribs too painful for it to continue.

An hour later, the cub watched Kimba tracking the pride and hid from him in a clump of thorn bush. Kimba passed close by but never saw it. He was too engrossed in following Cutlip's scent. After he had gone, the cub came out into the open and tried to run after him. Its cries did not carry very far.

Kimba followed the pride all that morning, taking great care not to be seen. He skirted round the shoulders of hills to avoid having to cross the skyline. It was much further to walk but it gave him a better chance of keeping the element of surprise. He found the place where the pride had rested during the afternoon. One of the cubs had been sick there. They had lain down under a clump of shady trees.

Both the males had sharpened their claws against the biggest tree. He found metre-long scratches on either side of the trunk. He studied the size of Cutlip and Tula's paw marks and the length of their stride. That depressed him.

He also found that Chem now led the pride with Sabba trailing some distance behind. By the time Kimba left, he knew the exact composition of the group and could guess at most of the changes that had happened. The pride was far more spread out than any other he had come across. He tucked that information away in the back of his mind. Some day it might be important.

He walked on, keeping in cover whenever possible. Towards late afternoon the ground became very broken with outcrops of rock and deep ravines plunging downwards. Kimba stopped and considered. He could see a long gully ahead of him leading up a steep-sided kopje.

He was certain the pride was up there. It was a good place to watch from. The gully he noticed became much narrower as it got higher. If Cutlip or Tula caught him there, he would be at their mercy. There was no point inviting danger. Kimba glanced at the sun and decided it was time to find a place to lie up in during the night. He had a final look at the kopje, then turned away.

There was another narrow track nearby and he followed it. He was suddenly weary and plodded along between thick patches of scrub. It was still very hot and the dust hung in the air long after he had passed. He sneezed and began to wonder what had happened to Meru. A lizard shot across his path. Ten metres ahead of him, a lion grunted.

Kimba froze, shocked. The grunt came again. A deep, throaty warning that brought the hair up along his spine. For a moment, he panicked. Cutlip had outflanked him. He must have known Kimba had been following the pride all the time. He had set a trap and Kimba had walked into it like a newborn zebra foal. He spun round. There was no sign of any other lion behind him. So Tula must be in the rocks somewhere above him ready to leap across his back and hold him down.

A branch shook and a bird shot out of a bush, its cry of warning shrilling behind it. The branch swayed and a lion stood blocking the path. It stared straight at him. It was Black Mane!

Fifteen

They stood looking at each other for a long time. Black Mane was much leaner and more scarred than the last time Kimba had seen him. There were deep claw marks across his rump and his ribs showed. But there was no mistaking the power of his shoulders and legs.

Kimba felt a fierce sense of elation at seeing him. Then, as Black Mane's steady gaze never left his face, he felt almost like a cub again. Kimba dropped his stare and looked at the ground. Black Mane gave a yawn and stretched, his paws ripping great furrows in the ground.

He gave a soft grunt of acceptance and Kimba approached him. Slowly, the younger lion came to within a metre of his sire. Then he was rubbing his head in Black Mane's chest and a rare feeling of happiness possessed him. Kio had been right. He was back with his own kind at last. For a moment, a flood of tenderness welled up inside him and threatened to get the better of his fierce nature. Perhaps Black Mane felt it too. He rubbed his shoulder along Kimba's body and afterwards stood silently beside him.

Kimba wanted to roar his defiance of Cutlip. He wanted to warn Tula of his own strength and power. But he didn't. He could sense Black Mane's insistence on silence. The older lion grunted and set out along the track, heading away from the kopje. Kimba followed a few metres behind. They walked in silence for three kilometres. Black Mane never paused or looked back.

Once they met an impala buck browsing in chest-high grass. It rolled its eyes and stood rooted to the spot in fear. Black Mane ignored it. After they had passed, Kimba looked back over his shoulder and saw the animal toss its horns and leap away.

They didn't stop until they reached Black Mane's favourite resting place. It was high up on a ridge between two hills. A tree gave good shade during the day and the river ran in the valley below. It was an excellent place to watch from. When they got there, Black Mane marked the tree and prowled round to see if any other lions had been there. Then he lay down and gave a huge yawn.

Kimba walked past the tree towards a clump of low bushes some fifty metres away. He could smell leopards and guessed that the tree was also much used by them.

He watched Black Mane and hesitated. What he was going to do next was very dangerous. He knew that. It could easily enrage the older lion and bring him charging across the open ground to drive him away for ever. But there was nothing Kimba could do to stop it. It was just nature and his instinct asserting itself.

He backed up against the bushes and marked them with his own scent. He looked over at Black Mane, ready to run for his life. He waited, then pretended to be engrossed in other smells. A few minutes later he approached the watching lion. He made himself walk in front of him as casually as he could. Black Mane grunted and laid his head on his paws.

Trying very hard not to show his nervousness, Kimba lay down a couple of metres away. Black Mane's eyes closed. Kimba lay as still as he could and hoped Black Mane could not hear the thumping of his heart. A fierce elation seized him. He had never felt such strength before. This acceptance by Black Mane changed everything. Now he really was a lion.

Black Mane woke two hours later. He went over and stood beside Kimba who grunted in understanding and followed him into the night.

They walked quickly, following their tracks back to the kopje. Black Mane stopped every hundred metres or so and marked the ground. Kimba did the same. They found the narrow path and silently padded upwards until they reached the sides of the kopje itself. Here they stopped and listened. They took care to stay in cover. The night was still and humid. There was a storm brewing to the north.

A family of baboons had settled for the night along the narrow ledges near the top of the kopje. Their scent clung to the wild banana trees at the bottom of the rocks. A stone came bouncing down and landed near Kimba. He heard a baboon scold its baby. He also heard the faint cry of a hungry cub and the louder snarl of an adult lion. He thought the lion was Tula. He sounded hungry and bad-tempered. Black Mane looked up at the rocks. He took a deep breath and roared. In the darkness, it was deafening. Kimba joined in. It was a wonderful sensation.

There was a startled reaction from overhead. Kimba heard Tula summoning Cutlip. Black Mane roared seven times in quick succession. He mocked Cutlip for hiding among the rocks like a dog-faced baboon, too frightened to go out hunting at night with the females.

Once he got over the shock of finding Black Mane and Kimba in the middle of his territory, Cutlip's rage was terrible. He and Tula roared and threatened continuously for the next half an hour.

But when they stopped, Black Mane and Kimba were still there, unafraid and challenging. Kimba thought he saw movement against the skyline, two long shapes moving between boulders. They waited until there was no doubt. Cutlip and Tula were coming down to fight. Kimba took a deep breath. The skin around his mouth grew tight.

But then, Black Mane did something totally unexpected. He turned, ran back for some distance along the path, marked the ground beside a tiny stream, leapt sideways and then followed along it. Kimba splashed after him. He had forgotten just how well Black Mane knew his old territory.

They skirted the sides of the hill for almost a kilometre until Black Mane found the gully he was looking for.

It was hard going even for a lion. In places the ground rose almost vertically. In others, they had to squeeze under great overhangs of rock. The baboons had fled a long time ago but there were fresh traces of them everywhere. Only sheer strength got the lions to the top. They came out on the far side of the kopje, panting with effort, and slumped down on a slab of bare rock. Below them, the plains spread for miles.

Along the horizon sheet lightning faded and glowed. It lit up great expanses of bush and the towering clouds above. The air was electric. Black Mane grunted in satisfaction. Chem was far below them and moving down on to the plain. Sabba and Pemba were following. Behind them came all the cubs. They saw Chem stop, her head on one side. Kimba tried to follow what she was looking at. He thought he saw a small herd of zebra but could not be sure. The lightning made it hard to be certain. Sabba and Pemba joined her. The cubs waited nearby. They watched Pemba leave the others and strike off to one side. So there was prey out there after all.

Kimba sat up and watched, totally absorbed. His

experienced eye plotted Pemba's likely course as he caught the odd glimpse of her. He watched the other lionesses and the cubs fan out into a ragged line.

There was a brilliant flash of lightning and Kimba thought he could see zebra galloping. It was difficult to tell in the flickering light. Thunder banged overhead and with it came more lightning. He saw Pemba racing towards the rest of the pride and knew she must be springing the trap. Now he could plainly see the zebras. They were bunching together in panic.

He watched Chem racing alongside them. Saw her jump. Her front legs stretching towards one. The next instant, she was falling and rolling over and over across the ground. The zebra had got in a hefty kick.

He saw Sabba hurl herself at a zebra's neck and bring it crashing down. Pemba came racing in and flung herself on its back. The zebra kicked frantically for a little and then was still.

Black Mane didn't wait a moment longer. He was on his feet and plunging down the hillside with Kimba running to keep up. They ran straight towards the kill, knowing that Cutlip and Tula were following the markings they had left and getting further away by the minute.

They heard Sabba roaring in triumph and Pemba joining in. Chem was back on her feet, bruised and winded but otherwise unhurt. She was far more upset by Sabba making the kill than by the pain of the zebra's kick. They listened to her snarling bad-temperedly.

As Black Mane and Kimba approached, they heard the lionesses starting to feed. Kimba's mouth watered. Hyenas were also appearing. There were already a dozen of them drifting in and out of the shadows, pressing closer to the kill. They had no idea that Black Mane and Kimba were so close. Black Mane bounded towards the zebra and burst into the middle of them, scattering hyenas, lions and cubs in all directions. The hyenas screamed and fled. Sabba and the others bolted into the bush, hardly knowing what was happening.

Kimba and Black Mane settled down at either end of the zebra and ate greedily.

The lionesses gathered their cubs together and after a long pause edged closer. It took Sabba a little while to realise that this was not Cutlip and Tula tearing at the carcass. These were other lions. Newcomers. She stared at them and then realised in total disbelief who they were. Black Mane and Kimba together! Alive! And challenging for the pride! She roared in excitement and was about to rush forward to greet them, when she heard Chem snarling at her.

It was a particularly nasty snarl. Sabba paused. She looked down at her little cubs and remembered how ruthless Cutlip was. Chem was another threat. Chem would kill them without any hesitation if there was any threat to her position. Sabba looked across at Black Mane and realised that there was no guarantee that he and Kimba would win. Sadly, she looked away and busied herself with the cubs.

Chem pushed past her. She started to pace up and down in front of Kimba and Black Mane. She was hungry, her cubs were starving but above all she was incensed at what had happened. Her growling grew louder. Now she was roaring for Cutlip and Tula to come and protect the pride. Black Mane looked up and bared his teeth at her.

Chem's anger made her grow bolder still. She roared her hatred of the two intruders. Her cubs growled with her. She came closer, her head bending towards the zebra. Then Black Mane was leaping across the kill at her and cuffing her a heavy blow to the head.

Chem staggered and fell over but recovered quickly

and rolled out of the way in one continuous movement. Black Mane started to chase after her, then gave up and came back to the kill. Pemba and Sabba waited until he had settled down again then reluctantly followed after Chem. The smell of zebra filled their nostrils. As they left, their cubs began to wail.

Chem walked for two hours and roared for most of the way. When she at last heard Cutlip answering, she was filled with fresh rage. Cutlip and Tula listened in disbelief while she told them what had happened. Cutlip had been tricked and made a fool of by Black Mane. Cutlip and Tula had failed the pride. Hyenas made better protectors! Sabba and Pemba stood behind her, scornful witnesses to the lions' shame. Chem was merciless. In the end, Cutlip bit her ear and slashed her back.

But they could still hear her roars of contempt later that night, as they followed Black Mane's tracks. They had found the zebra, but what little was left of it the scavengers were finishing.

Cutlip and Tula swallowed their hunger and walked in silence a few metres apart. The smell of fresh zebra blood hung easily in the warm night air. They had no trouble following their enemy.

The sky was getting lighter in the east as they approached the river. Cutlip knew it would be dawn by the time they got there. He guessed that Black Mane and Kimba would be sleeping it off by now. When they woke, they would feel heavy and their reactions would be much slower than usual.

It was a perfect time to catch them. He remembered to keep the sun behind him when he attacked . . .

Sixteen

The sun rose in a great flaming ball. It cleared the horizon and flooded the plains with a blinding light. The antelope herds tossed their heads in the sudden warmth and stamped their feet. They looked round at each other, glad the night was over.

In the river, Kirek the crocodile lay very still. Only the top of his nostrils and his eyes showed. His tail moved very slightly to counter the current. He could feel the flow pushing at his jaws. He was waiting. For the past three mornings, a flock of wild goats had come to this same spot to drink. He had studied them carefully. Today, he would seize one and take it down to the larder of dead things he kept at the bottom of the river.

The goats were late. Kirek moved his massive head to one side, listening for the sharp rap of their hooves on the hard-packed earth. Something moved above him. He looked up and knew they would not be coming. A lion stood there, staring at the river. As Kirek watched, it shook itself and came down the steep slope of the bank to drink.

Kimba hadn't seen the crocodile. He knew it was there somewhere, but the glare off the river made it impossible to see. He was also very thirsty. He squinted into the sun for a moment then bent down and started to drink.

The crocodile was not the only animal watching Kimba. Fifty metres away, Cutlip and Tula stood motionless in the undergrowth, barely able to restrain their excitement. They had found both Black Mane and Kimba stretched out fast asleep under a tree two hundred metres back from the river. Cutlip was on the point of attacking them then and there, when Kimba woke up and headed sleepily for the river.

Cutlip and Tula followed at a discreet distance. They could hardly believe their luck. Together, they would now give Kimba a beating he would never forget. Then they would go back and finish off the sleeping Black Mane.

They noticed the bole of a dead palm tree immediately above the spot where Kimba was drinking. It made a perfect marker. Like a shadow, Tula slipped away. He kept his eyes fixed on the tree and stayed out of sight. It took barely thirty seconds to get there. He dropped down behind it and very carefully crawled forward. For a second Tula looked down on the unsuspecting Kimba. Then he glanced further down the river and saw Cutlip waiting. Tula drew back, gathered himself and sprang down the bank.

With a great leap, Tula landed full-length on top of the unsuspecting lion just as Kimba stood up. Tula's impact carried him tumbling over Kimba's shoulders. He splashed head-first into the river, swallowed a mouthful of water and came up choking. It gave Kimba barely enough time to recover.

Winded and taken totally by surprise, Kimba struggled to get up. He was lucky. Two seconds earlier and the impact would have broken his back. It was still bad enough. He was fighting for breath but the muscles of his body refused to work. In a haze of agony, he saw Tula only two metres away and turning towards him. If Tula was here, Cutlip could not be far away. Kimba's back was unprotected, open to Cutlip's crushing bite.

It was sheer terror that got Kimba up in time. He was staggering, his breath coming in great gasps but at last he was on his feet. There was a snarl of triumph behind him and Cutlip stood there. He threw back his head and roared then leapt at Kimba.

For a tiny instant, the sun shone straight into his eyes, blinding him as he landed. Cutlip hesitated for a second too long. Kimba hurled himself at Cutlip, biting down hard into the muscle of his back.

Cutlip roared and twisted round to swipe at Kimba. The blows from his great paws thudded into Kimba's head and neck. Blood was streaming across Kimba's shoulders. But still he held on. He had the advantage and he knew it. His back legs kicked and he twisted his head to bite deeper. He heard the fear in Cutlip's roars.

Cutlip stumbled and fell, breaking Kimba's deadly grip. Tula lunged at his throat. Kimba swayed back and hit him a huge blow across the nose as Tula overbalanced.

Out of the corner of his eye, Kimba saw Cutlip coming for him. Kimba rolled over on his back like a cat and confronted them with every weapon he possessed. It was a last desperate defence. Tula slashed down at his eyes. Kimba took the blow on his scarred front leg. Cutlip was towering above him on the other side. Tula struck again. Kimba rolled slightly to meet him. Quick as a flash Cutlip's head thudded into the back of his ribs, trying to push him over.

Kimba tried to get back but Cutlip was too strong. Inch by inch Cutlip was forcing him over. Tula's claws shot out and ripped at his ear. Cutlip was snarling in triumph and Kimba knew he couldn't last much longer.

There was more noise and roaring all around him. In despair, Kimba turned his head and saw Black Mane standing beside him. Cutlip backed away. Kimba heaved himself upright and for a moment thought his legs were going to buckle under him. He had never felt so tired. There were deep teeth marks in his back leg, but he couldn't remember being bitten.

Kimba knew he must ignore everything. Cutlip and Tula were far from beaten. As if reading his thoughts, Black Mane challenged them both. Cutlip roared back and began to strut forward. His mane stood up round his head. His tail rose high over his back. They met head on, clutching each other by the shoulders and struggling upright, biting and snarling and cuffing the other round the head.

Cutlip caught Black Mane two tremendous blows before Black Mane side-stepped and lunged at Cutlip's throat. Cutlip dodged, reared up and fell across Black

Mane's shoulders. Now he was a dead weight forcing Black Mane down on to the sand.

Before Kimba could move, Tula was running in and slashing at Black Mane's back legs, trying to cut the tendons and lame him. Black Mane staggered towards the river, roaring for help.

Kimba ran at Tula from behind, took him by surprise and bit hard. Tula howled and dodged back into the river. Suddenly, there was a lot of blood in the water. Tula stayed there, chest deep and snarling in pain.

With an imperceptible sweep of his tail, Kirek eased forward. Two more powerful thrusts and he was gliding across the river towards them. With infinite care he floated closer. He was very near now, the energy for the attack building inside him.

Cutlip heard Tula's distress and hesitated. Black Mane felt his indecision and slid him off his shoulders. Cutlip landed on his feet and backed away.

He watched Black Mane and Kimba closing in on him. He roared at them to keep back and looked quickly round. Tula was badly hurt. He could no longer fight. The only way out now was to swim to the far bank. He grunted at Tula.

As Tula turned to flee, Kirek swung his tail in two powerful heaves, dug deeply with his back legs and, with jaws gaping, came up out of the river in one terrible movement. For a moment, the crocodile hung over Tula. Then, seizing him by the head, Kirek fell back in an explosion of spray and dragged the lion with him. The surface boiled as Kirek rolled over on top of Tula, driving the air from his lungs in great bursting bubbles. A little later, they both sank from view.

Black Mane and Kimba stood rooted to the spot, unable to believe what they had seen. Cutlip's reactions were much quicker. He had felt the crocodile slide past him and seen Tula in its mouth. He was out of the water and racing for his life before the other lions realised he had gone.

They stared at the surface for a long time, then turned and silently made their way back to the safety of the bush.

Kimba and Black Mane lay up all that day under a tree. They licked their wounds and tried to sleep. But every time Kimba dozed, his dreams were full of Cutlip, Tula and the crocodile, waiting to drag him back into the water.

For a while, they were plagued by a troop of monkeys who threw fruit stones at them and then sat in the branches screaming. Eventually the monkeys grew bored and left. Kimba woke after another nightmare and found himself shivering uncontrollably. He sat up and saw a cloud of flies feeding on the gashes along Black Mane's side. Black Mane's mouth was twitching and his legs jerked. Kimba guessed that he too was remembering what had happened.

They left the river at dusk, Kimba hobbling and trying not to put any weight on his injured leg. Black Mane led the way. They were stiff and very bruised and for the first hour, progress was slow. A pack of wild dogs saw them and began to follow. The dogs could smell the fresh blood oozing from their wounds. Black Mane chased one that came too close. It yelped and dodged away. The next time Kimba looked round they had all gone.

A herd of wildebeest saw them coming and parted to let them through. They climbed up to the solitary tree on the ridge. When they got there, they sat down side by side and began to roar. Every few minutes, they stopped to listen.

Sometime after midnight, they heard an answering roar. Gradually it came nearer. More lions were joining in. It was the pride. Their pride! Black Mane and Kimba were almost hoarse with excitement by the time the pride came up the hill to join them.

Sabba came first. She rubbed heads with Black

Mane and then with Kimba. Pemba was next, followed by Wheen and Kitu and Pemba's cubs. The new males, Black Mane and Kimba, drew themselves up to their full height, their wounds forgotten.

Last of all came Chem. She had been standing to one side, watching silently. But later, when Kimba looked for her, she had gone and taken her cubs with her.

Later still, Sabba took the pride out hunting. As luck would have it, they made two good kills not far from the ridge. She called Black Mane and Kimba to join them and they fed until dawn.

The sun climbed higher and both Kimba and Black Mane began to yawn. The events of the last twenty-four hours were catching up with them with a vengeance.

They followed Sabba up M'goma Hill to the shade of the rocks. Wearily, Kimba flopped down and yawned again. Pemba's cubs had found a grasshopper and were trying to catch it.

Kimba's eyes kept closing. He was aware of Sabba standing beside him, purring with pleasure. He wanted to sit up and rub heads with her. He would after he had slept. Life was suddenly very good again . . .